TOAD SURPRISE

Morris Gleitzman

Puffin Books

PUFFIN BOOKS

Published by the Penguin Group
Penguin Group (Australia)
250 Camberwell Road
Camberwell, Victoria 3124, Australia
(a division of Pearson Australia Group Pty Ltd)
Penguin Group (USA) Inc.
375 Hudson Street, New York, New York 10014, USA
Penguin Group (Canada)
90 Eglinton Avenue East, Suite 700,
Toronto ON M4P 2Y3, Canada
(a division of Pearson Penguin Canada Inc.)
Penguin Books Ltd
80 Strand, London WC2R 0RL, England
Penguin Ireland
25 St Stephen's Green, Dublin 2, Ireland
(a division of Penguin Books Ltd)
Penguin Books India Pvt Ltd
11, Community Centre, Panchsheel Park, New Delhi -110 017, India
Penguin Group (NZ)
67 Apollo Drive, Rosedale, North Shore 0632, New Zealand
(a division of Pearson New Zealand Ltd)
Penguin Books (South Africa) (Pty) Ltd
24 Sturdee Avenue, Rosebank, Johannesburg 2196, South Africa

Penguin Books Ltd, Registered Offices: 80 Strand, London WC2R 0RL, England

First published by Penguin Group (Australia), 2008

1 3 5 7 9 10 8 6 4 2

Cover design by Elissa Christian © Penguin Group (Australia)
Illustrations by Rod Clement
Typeset in 13/15pt Minion by Post Pre-Press Group, Brisbane, Queensland
Printed and bound in Australia by McPherson's Printing Group, Maryborough, Victoria

National Library of Australia
Cataloguing-in-Publication data:

Gleitzman, Morris, 1953– .
Toad surprise / Morris Gleitzman.

ISBN: 978 0 14 330416 6.

A823.3

puffin.com.au

Eck
From
Fletcher &
Darcy

PUFFIN BOOKS

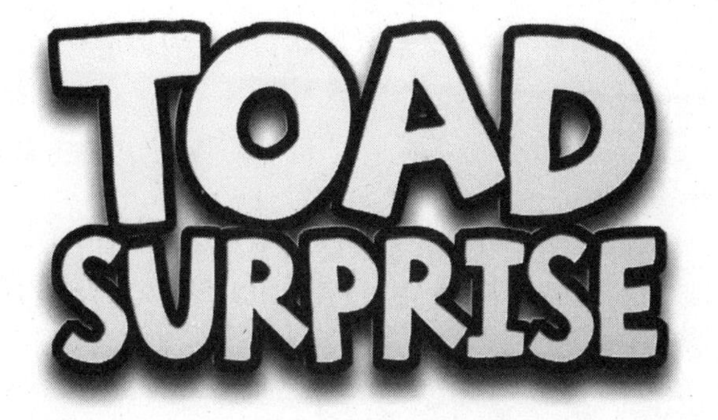

Stack Me!

It's the wart-tingling
escapade of one slightly squashed
cane toad's hunt for friendship
and the surprising place
he finds it.

Also by Morris Gleitzman

Toad Rage
Toad Heaven
Toad Away
The Other Facts of Life
Second Childhood
Two Weeks with the Queen
Misery Guts
Worry Warts
Puppy Fat
Blabber Mouth
Sticky Beak
Gift of the Gab
Belly Flop
Water Wings
Wicked! (with Paul Jennings)
Deadly! (with Paul Jennings)
Bumface
Adults Only
Teacher's Pet
Boy Overboard
Girl Underground
Worm Story
Aristotle's Nostril
Doubting Thomas
Give Peas a Chance
Once
Then

For Lilly, Maggie, Baddie,
Deeks, Max and Kitmas

'Danger,' yelled Limpy. 'Everyone off the road.'

It was dinner time in North Queensland. On the highway, in the glowing dusk, cane toads were munching contentedly. And burping a bit. All except for Limpy, who was hopping up and down on top of an ant hill, waving frantically at the others.

'Please,' he begged them. 'Move.'

The other cane toads on the highway didn't move. They didn't even look up.

Oh no, realised Limpy, they can't hear me.

He knew why. It was because they were such noisy eaters. And their dinners were even noisier. The air was full of flying insects complaining loudly about being eaten.

Limpy pointed to the headlights in the distance.

'Truck coming,' he yelled.

It was no good.

Down on the road, his relatives couldn't see what

he could see up on the ant hill. They just carried on munching, unaware that sixteen wheels were about to hurtle round the bend in the highway and seriously flatten their warts.

Limpy's warts were prickling with panic. If his rellies didn't shift their buttocks soon, they'd be wearing them as eyebrows.

'Please,' Limpy begged his rellies again. 'Move.'

A flying insect stuck its head out of a cane toad's mouth and caught sight of Limpy's desperate hopping and waving.

'Hey, you lot,' yelled the flying insect. 'Pay attention. That young bloke's telling you to stop scoffing us and get off the road.'

Other flying insects saw Limpy and started yelling at the cane toads too. Slowly, the rellies got the message. They began to hop off the highway, still chewing.

But it was too late.

The truck roared round the bend and suddenly its huge headlights turned dusk into day.

Limpy stared in horror.

Several cane toads were still on the road, huddled together, chewing as fast as they could.

Oh no, thought Limpy.

He knew what would happen next.

It did.

The truck swerved across the road, directly towards the now trembling cane toads, and drove over them.

Pop. Pop. Pop. Pop.

Limpy couldn't look. He'd seen the horrible sight too often before. Plump happy rellies suddenly turned into tragic patches of flat skin and even flatter warts.

By a human.

On purpose.

Limpy moaned and slumped onto the ant hill.

'Excuse me,' said an annoyed voice.

Limpy looked around.

An ant was glaring at him.

'Would you mind not making so much noise on our roof,' said the ant. 'We're trying to get the kids to bed.'

It was a fair enough request. When Limpy had asked the ants if he could use their hill as a lookout, they'd said yes as long as he didn't eat them afterwards or keep their kids awake.

'Sorry,' said Limpy. 'I forgot.'

The ant peered down at the squashed rellies on the highway and gave Limpy a sympathetic look.

'Apology accepted,' said the ant. 'Bad luck about that lot. Still, three or four's not as bad as it used to be before you had the lookout, eh?'

Limpy sighed.

The ant was right, but it didn't make him feel any better.

'We're very grateful for the use of the roof,' said Limpy. 'If there's anything we can do in return, just let us know. Your kids are welcome to use our mud slide. And if you ever need repairs done to your hill, my cousin Goliath can carry huge amounts of mud in his mouth.'

While the ant was thinking about this, Limpy saw something out of the corner of his eye that made him forget all about roof repairs.

Another vehicle was coming.

And a toad was still squatting out in the middle of the highway.

Limpy could tell instantly who it was from the big muscly shoulders silhouetted in the headlights. And the big muscly arms. And the stick the toad was waving above his big muscly head.

Goliath.

'Thanks again,' said Limpy hastily to the ant, and hopped off the ant hill. He hit ground so hard he felt like he'd dented several warts, but he hurried onto the highway towards Goliath.

Not too fast, Limpy reminded himself.

That was the worst thing about having a crook leg. Try to hop too fast and you just went round in circles. Which wasn't so good when you were trying to rescue a stubborn rellie from certain death.

'Goliath,' shouted Limpy as he got nearer to his cousin. 'Don't do it. Get off the road.'

'Don't try to stop me,' said Goliath, glaring into the approaching headlights. 'Those mongrel humans have pushed us around for too long. Well this is showdown time. I'm an angry cane toad and I've got a stick.'

Limpy felt weak with panic.

Arguing with Goliath was pointless. When he got an idea in his head, not even a large rock would shift it.

Limpy grabbed Goliath's big arm and tried to drag him off the highway. But Goliath was too heavy. Limpy couldn't even drag Goliath off the white line.

'Mongrel,' Goliath was yelling at the vehicle. 'I'm gunna pop your tyres and stab your wheel rims.'

The vehicle was so close now that Limpy could feel the heat from the headlights.

Suddenly he knew this was it.

The moment he'd always feared. The moment he and poor Goliath would end up flat and dead, just like all the sun-dried rellies Limpy had spent his life hauling off the highway and carrying home and stacking neatly in his bedroom, one stack for uncles, one for aunties, one for cousins and one for their popped-off warts.

No point running now. Cane toads weren't as fast as vehicles, and vehicles could swerve all over the road when there was squashing to be done. It was a law of nature.

Limpy blinked in the glare of the headlights. For a moment he felt a pang of regret that he'd never achieved his life's ambition – friendship between humans and cane toads.

He made sure that his last thought was about Mum and Dad and Charm and how much he loved them and how lucky he was to have a sister who knew how to reassemble a squashed cane toad's buttocks after he was dead.

Then an amazing thing happened.

So amazing, Limpy couldn't believe it even as he watched it.

The vehicle swerved, but not towards him and Goliath.

Away from them.

The driver must have hit the brakes because suddenly the tyres were squealing. As the ute skidded past, the wind from it was so strong that Limpy felt his face being pulled out of shape.

His brain felt pulled out of shape too.

With amazement.

Limpy had never seen this before.

A human driver trying on purpose *not* to kill a cane toad.

Limpy watched, stunned, as the ute slewed off the highway and came to a sudden stop in the long grass, not far from the ant hill.

Goliath was looking pretty stunned too.

'I won,' he croaked, staring at his stick in a dazed sort of way. 'Unreal.'

'It's more than unreal,' said Limpy. 'That human has just done the most amazing thing in the history of cane toads.'

Goliath scowled at the ute in the long grass.

'That's not amazing,' he said. 'That's just bad parking.'

'Come on,' said Limpy. 'I hope the human's not hurt.'

Limpy hopped over to the edge of the highway and cautiously approached the ute through the grass.

He could hear Goliath following close behind.

'If the human isn't hurt now,' muttered Goliath, 'he will be as soon as I can sharpen this stick. And as soon as you give me a leg up so I can reach his belly button.'

Limpy gave Goliath a look.

'I don't want you to even think about hurting him,' said Limpy. 'Because what you are about to see is something you've never seen before.'

Goliath frowned. 'Dung beetles using deodorant?'

'A human driver,' said Limpy, 'who doesn't hate cane toads.'

Goliath stared at Limpy and snorted. 'No such thing.'

But Limpy knew there was. He'd seen it with his own eyes.

And now, as he watched the driver's door swing open and two legs appear, a hopeful glow spread through his warts. Was is possible that this human might be able to help him achieve his life's ambition?

Friendship between humans and cane toads, with no killing.

Limpy didn't say anything to Goliath.

It was probably a silly thought.

But as the rest of the human emerged from the ute, the thought suddenly didn't seem so silly after all.

'What?' said Goliath nervously.

Limpy realised he was squeezing one of Goliath's warts very hard with excitement as he gazed up at the human.

At the big black boots.

At the red jacket and pants.

At the long white beard.

'Stack me,' said Limpy. 'I think I know who this is.'

'Limpy,' said Mum, frowning. 'Slow down. You know you're not meant to hop fast in here.'

'Sorry, Mum,' panted Limpy as he hopped very fast towards his room.

Suddenly his crook leg gave way. He swerved and crashed into Dad, who was helping Mum peel lizards.

'Sorry, Dad,' said Limpy.

Dad helped Limpy up.

Limpy picked a lizard spleen off Dad's head.

'For swamp's sake, Limpy,' said Dad. 'I know you can't help your leg, but that's it, you're grounded. No mud slide for three nights. And if you weren't our only surviving son, I'd make it six.'

Limpy didn't argue. There wasn't time.

If I'm right about the human in the ute, he thought, Mum and Dad will understand why I'm in such a rush.

'Come and mash these slugs for me,' said Mum.

'Sorry, can't right now,' said Limpy. 'I have to urgently identify a human.'

Limpy hurried, not quite so fast, through the tropical leaves into his room. He rummaged behind the stacks of flat sun-dried rellies next to his bed and found what he was looking for.

His human newspapers.

Limpy didn't keep much of the stuff that was chucked from passing cars or left at picnic grounds, but he always kept the magazines and newspapers. They were the best thing ever for understanding humans.

He unfolded one of the newspapers and started turning the pages.

It wasn't easy. The newspaper filled his room and Limpy had to hang off the creepers growing across his ceiling and turn the pages from there.

Suddenly his leg slipped and he crashed down onto a page.

And there it was, right under his nose, clear as anything in the moonlight coming through the creepers – the ad he was looking for.

Yes, he thought.

I'm right.

It is him.

There was a crackling and rustling at the edge of the page.

Mum's head appeared, then Dad's.

'What do you mean, identify a human?' said Dad.

'Goliath's not trying to eat one, is he?' said Mum.

Limpy shook his head.

'Look,' he said excitedly, pointing to the page.

Mum and Dad hopped onto the newspaper and stood next to Limpy, staring down at the human in the ad.

At the big black boots.

At the red jacket and pants.

At the long white beard and friendly twinkling eyes.

'He's called Santa,' said Limpy. 'A Christmas beetle told me about him. Santa is the nicest human in the whole world. He fills the hearts of other humans with peace and goodwill.'

Mum looked doubtful.

'I'd like to see that,' she said.

'It's true,' said Limpy.

'What are those weird animals?' said Dad, pointing to the ad. 'Why have they got tree branches growing out of their heads?'

'They're called reindeer,' said Limpy. 'They're Santa's helpers. Humans are very fond of reindeer. I reckon if a cane toad was Santa's helper, humans would be fond of us too.'

Limpy watched as Mum and Dad took this in.

'Why are you telling us this?' said Dad.

'Santa's down at the highway right now,' said Limpy. 'With Goliath.'

Mum and Dad stared at Limpy.

Limpy took a deep breath and explained the whole thing, right up to the best bit where Santa swerved off the road because of all the peace and goodwill in his heart.

'Goliath's trying to stop Santa leaving,' said Limpy. 'Until I can get back there.'

Mum and Dad exchanged a look.

'Limpy,' said Mum. 'Be honest with us. Are you about to go on another dangerous quest to try and bring safety and happiness to cane toads for countless generations to come?'

Limpy knew Mum and Dad probably wouldn't like the idea. Parents never did if it involved risking your life, specially when you were grounded. But Limpy decided to tell them the truth.

'Yes, I am,' he said. 'If I can be Santa's helper, I think it'll change the way humans feel about cane toads.'

Mum and Dad looked at each other again.

Then they both gave Limpy long hugs.

'Be careful,' whispered Mum. 'And come home soon.'

'Don't worry, Mum,' said Limpy. 'I will.'

'We're proud of you, son,' said Dad. 'Good luck.'

'Thanks, Dad,' said Limpy.

'Remember,' said Mum. 'No fast hopping.'

Limpy gave Mum and Dad one last hug, then headed off. There were a couple of things he had to do before he clambered on board Santa's ute. And keeping busy was the best way not to feel sad about leaving.

'Limpy,' called Dad.

Limpy stopped and turned.

'Yes?' he said.

'You're not grounded any more,' said Dad.

On the way back to Santa, Limpy visited the Christmas beetle for advice.

Limpy knew it had to be a quick visit because Santa wouldn't stay stuck in the long grass for ever. Not even if Goliath had managed to let the air out of Santa's tyres and stuff swamp slime up Santa's exhaust pipe.

'Go away,' said the Christmas beetle, glaring down at Limpy from a leaf overhanging the moonlit swamp. 'I'm not on duty. Christmas isn't for another two days.'

Limpy blinked.

This was a bit too quick.

'I promise I won't take up much of your time, Mr Christmas Beetle,' he said. 'I just need to ask you about Santa.'

The Christmas beetle scowled and muttered things that Limpy was pretty sure didn't have much to do with Christmas peace and goodwill.

'If I've told you kids once,' said the Christmas beetle crossly, 'I've told you a million times. Santa only brings presents for humans. He does not bring presents for ants, lizards, mice, fruit bats, snakes, termites, echidnas, wombats, slugs, toads or, I'm sorry to say, Christmas beetles.'

'Actually,' said Limpy. 'I was hoping you could

give me some advicc. About being Santa's helper.'

The Christmas beetle stared at Limpy.

'You?' said the Christmas beetle. 'Santa's helper? Don't even think about it.'

'Why not?' said Limpy.

'Because,' said the Christmas beetle, 'Santa only employs top professionals, not daydreaming dill-brains.'

Limpy ignored the unkind comment.

'Everyone has to start somewhere,' he said. 'With a bit of experience I could be a top professional.'

'Yeah, right,' said the Christmas beetle. 'You want to start somewhere? Here's where you can start. Put your hand on your head.'

Limpy was puzzled, but he did it anyway.

'OK,' said the Christmas beetle. 'Can you feel any tree branches growing out of your skull?'

Limpy couldn't.

'Which means,' said the Christmas beetle, 'you're not a reindeer, you're a cane toad. So my advice is, forget the whole idea.'

Limpy thought about this.

It wasn't really the advice he'd hoped for.

'I can't forget the whole idea,' said Limpy. 'There are too many lives at stake.'

The Christmas beetle stopped rolling his eyes and muttering things about witless wart-brains, and looked at Limpy.

'That's why I need to be Santa's helper,' Limpy went on. 'So humans will feel Christmas peace and goodwill towards all cane toads and stop killing us.'

The Christmas beetle thought about this.

Limpy wondered whether to tell the Christmas beetle about Santa being in the long grass next to the highway.

He decided not to. There wasn't time.

'If you stop bugging me,' said the Christmas beetle, 'I'll tell you what you need to know. Santa lives very far away in a place called the North Pole. The whole joint is covered in freezing white stuff called snow. Well, some of it's actually reindeer dandruff, but it's still extremely cold. So my advice is, if by some miracle you end up there, don't stay long or you'll die.'

'Thank you,' said Limpy gratefully.

He headed off towards the highway.

That was exactly the sort of useful advice he'd been hoping for.

'The North Pole?' said Charm.

Her eyes, glowing green in the moonlight, were wide with concern.

Limpy, crouched next to her behind some swamp weed, tried to look like going to the North Pole wasn't a big deal.

He wasn't surprised Charm was concerned. It was her loving nature. Plus little sisters often got a bit concerned about older brothers possibly freezing their warts off.

'I'll probably only go to the North Pole for tonight,' said Limpy. 'Then tomorrow, which is Christmas Eve, I'll be travelling all over the world delivering presents to human children.'

Charm looked even more concerned. She put her arms round Limpy and pressed her cheek against his tummy.

'It sounds very dangerous,' she said.

Limpy gave his little sister a loving squeeze to let

her know it was going to be completely safe.

'I won't be there long enough to freeze to death,' he said.

Charm didn't look convinced.

'What if you get eaten by a reindeer?' she said.

'Reindeer are vegetarian,' said Limpy, but he wasn't completely sure about that.

Charm was starting to make him feel a bit nervous. He pushed his fears and the swamp weed aside and peered over at Santa's ute. The rear wheels were spinning in the mud as Santa tried to reverse back onto the highway.

Goliath, hunched in the long grass near the ute, was peeing on the wheels to make the ground under them even muddier.

Good on you, Goliath, thought Limpy.

Goliath might not be the smartest cane toad in the swamp, but he was brilliant with mud.

Charm was frowning.

'I thought you said Santa flies around the world on a sleigh,' she said to Limpy. 'That looks more like a Commodore ute.'

'I know,' said Limpy. 'Maybe he prefers it for going to the shops.'

They watched as Santa stopped revving the ute, got out, pulled some branches off a bush and stuffed them under his rear wheels.

'That must be for grip,' said Limpy. 'He'll probably be out of the mud soon. I'd better get on board.'

'Limpy,' said Charm. 'I want to come too.'

Limpy looked at her dear little warty face.

He'd been expecting this.

Charm was incredibly brave for someone whose body hadn't grown properly because of pollution. Now, somehow, he had to find a way of persuading her to stay. Of making her see she was the only one who could take over lookout duty on the ant hill.

'But I'm not going to come,' said Charm.

'Eh?' said Limpy.

'Somebody has to do lookout duty on the ant hill,' said Charm. 'With you away it'd have to be me or Goliath. And Goliath would probably just eat the ants.'

Limpy had to agree with that.

'But I don't want you to go on your own,' continued Charm. 'So you have to take Goliath.'

Limpy opened his mouth to tell Charm all the reasons why that wouldn't be a good idea. Then he saw the expression on her face. Even her warts looked determined.

Limpy stared across at Goliath, who was punching himself in the stomach, trying to get a few more drops of pee out.

'You either have to take him or me,' said Charm.

Limpy sighed.

He didn't really have a choice.

'I'll take Goliath,' he said.

'And,' said Charm, 'you also have to take Uncle Vasco.'

Limpy stared at her as she rolled something out

of the swamp weed. It was poor flat Uncle Vasco, all sun-baked skin and squashed warts and vicious tyre marks. Limpy had been meaning to add Uncle Vasco to the uncle pile in his room for several days now, but hadn't got around to it.

'Please,' said Charm. 'You have to take him.'

Limpy didn't understand. Why did Charm want him to take an uncle who was flat and dead?

Then Limpy remembered that Uncle Vasco had always wanted to travel. That's how he'd got run over. He was on his way to the other side of the highway for a holiday, and turned round to wave goodbye just as a truck was coming.

'Charm,' said Limpy gently. 'How about if I promise to take Uncle Vasco on a holiday another time?'

Charm shook her head.

'You're not taking him on a holiday,' she said. 'You're taking him to keep you safe. So you won't forget what humans can do to cane toads. So if you're in danger, you'll be careful.'

Limpy saw that his sister's expression was loving and concerned, but also fierce and stubborn.

He sighed.

Oh well. At least having Uncle Vasco around might remind Goliath not to try wrestling any trucks at the North Pole.

Charm put her arms round Limpy's tummy again.

'I love you, Limpy,' she whispered. 'Be careful.'

'I love you too,' said Limpy.

He gave Charm one last hug, then heaved Uncle Vasco onto his shoulders and hopped towards Santa's ute before all the sad goodbye feelings made his crook leg go wobbly.

Riding in the back of Santa's ute wasn't very comfortable. The jolting and bumping were making Limpy's whole body feel battered, specially his warts.

Limpy wondered if warts ever just dropped off.

To take his mind off that possibility, Limpy gazed up at the moon and the dark trees flashing past. Also flashing past in the warm night air were flying insects, pulling faces and poking their tongues out at him and Goliath.

Goliath was trying to catch them in his mouth, but the air was rushing past too quickly.

'Nah, nah,' the flying insects were chortling. 'Missed us.'

'If we're Santa's helpers,' grumbled Goliath to Limpy, 'why are we getting sore bottoms bouncing around here in the back? Why aren't we riding up front with Santa, swapping reindeer jokes and snacking on Christmas beetles?'

‘I don’t think Santa eats Christmas beetles,’ said Limpy. ‘Plus it’s better if we stay hidden till we get to the North Pole.’

‘Why?’ frowned Goliath. ‘We don’t have to be scared of Santa. He’s totally into peace and goodwill. It’s not like he’s gunna beat us to death with big heavy presents or anything.’

‘I know,’ replied Limpy. ‘But we mustn’t rush into this. Just cause we’re volunteering doesn’t mean we’ll get the job. We have to wait till we can show Santa what good helpers we are.’

‘Why can’t we show him now?’ grumbled Goliath. ‘Why don’t we just go into that cab and pick the nits out of his beard and squeeze a couple of his pimples?’

Limpy shook his head.

‘It’s better if we wait till we get to the North Pole,’ he said. ‘That’s where Santa needs help most. With his workshop and his sleigh.’

‘And his pimples,’ muttered Goliath.

The ute swerved. Limpy found himself rolling across the hard metal floor.

He ended up on his back in a corner. He felt bruised, but he didn’t mind at all.

‘Did you feel that?’ he said to Goliath. ‘Santa must have swerved so we wouldn’t hit a rellie on the road. This is so exciting. I can’t believe we’ve found a human who feels peace and goodwill to all cane toads.’

Goliath grunted.

Limpy tried to pick himself up, but the ute did another swerve and he started to roll again. He saw that Uncle Vasco was rolling around too, which wasn't good. Flat sun-dried rellies could chip easily.

'Goliath,' said Limpy. 'Can you grab Uncle Vasco, please?'

Goliath grabbed Uncle Vasco.

Limpy managed to snatch hold of a big coil of rope. He clung on, wishing he was as strong and heavy as Goliath, who was hardly rolling around at all.

'When we get to the North Pole,' said Goliath, 'I'm gunna show Santa how good I am at arm wrestling.'

'Goliath,' begged Limpy. 'Please try and remember that Santa's helpers never attack Santa or any of his other helpers.'

Goliath scowled.

'Mongrel reindeer,' he said. 'If those twig-heads give us any trouble, I'm gunna build a tree house between their ears.'

Limpy felt a stab of concern.

Maybe bringing Goliath on a mission of peace and goodwill was as crazy as he'd feared. Maybe it could only end one way – with millions of angry humans and a sobbing Santa.

Limpy told himself to calm down.

He watched the way Goliath was lovingly picking grit out of Uncle Vasco's flattened nostrils.

Goliath's not so bad really, thought Limpy. I'd

probably feel a bit violent myself if humans had run over my parents.

The important thing, Limpy knew, was that underneath Goliath's grumpy warts and all the teeth marks on his tummy from fighting wombats there was a warm and loving heart.

Goliath scowled.

'When I see poor Uncle Vasco like this,' he said, licking one of Uncle Vasco's eyelids and sticking it back on, 'it makes me want to put prickly pear shrubs up humans' bottoms.'

Well, a fairly warm and loving heart.

'Try to have some peaceful Christmas thoughts,' said Limpy. 'And get some rest. Once we arrive at the North Pole, we're going to be very busy.'

While Goliath dozed with his arms round Uncle Vasco, Limpy hung onto the rope and gazed up at the distant stars and wondered if Santa delivered presents there as well.

Human technology is amazing, he thought. Camping chairs that fold up, newspapers with colour pictures, sleighs that can fly . . .

Limpy closed his eyes.

The vibration of the ute on the highway was quite relaxing now. It sounded a bit like when Dad hummed to himself with a mouthful of swamp slugs.

'Mmm,' said Goliath's sleepy voice. 'I know what I want for Christmas.'

'What?' murmured Limpy.

'Pizza,' said Goliath.

Limpy smiled.

Once this mission was a success, and humans started feeling peace and goodwill towards cane toads, and liking cane toads, and being friendly with cane toads, humans and cane toads would share heaps of pizzas together.

Now that, thought Limpy, is what I want for Christmas.

Limpy stood in the back of the ute, staring around him, warts tingling with amazement.

The North Pole didn't look anything like he'd imagined.

The palm trees were a surprise for a start.

And the streetlights.

And the parked cars.

Limpy couldn't see a single flake of frozen white stuff anywhere, and he could see all the way down the street to the video shop on the corner.

The ute came to a stop at the kerb and Goliath woke up.

'Are we there yet?' he mumbled.

'I think so,' whispered Limpy. 'Quick, hide.'

The driver's door was opening and Santa was getting out. Limpy grabbed Goliath and pulled him down behind a petrol can.

'Why are we hiding?' said Goliath. 'Why aren't we helping?'

‘We’re checking things out,’ said Limpy. ‘We’re looking for something to help with.’

He wondered if the petrol in the can might be some kind of special Christmas fuel. And whether they could help Santa fill up the fuel tank of the sleigh, which was probably parked just around the corner.

But Santa didn’t even give the back of the ute a glance.

Limpy watched as Santa had a stretch, scratched his beard, pulled the seat of his red pants out of his bottom crack, and walked up the path towards his workshop, which actually looked more like a fibro house with a wonky TV aerial on the roof.

‘I hope the North Pole has got insects and worms and pizza,’ said Goliath. ‘I’m starving.’

‘We can eat later,’ said Limpy. ‘First we have to show Santa what good helpers we are.’

Limpy checked that poor flat Uncle Vasco was safely hidden under the coil of rope. Then he clambered down the side of the ute to the footpath.

Goliath followed, grumbling.

They waited until Santa had found his key and gone into his workshop, then they crept up the path towards the front door.

‘Grrrrr!’

Limpy’s insides went stiff with fright.

Through a gap in the fence, an angry face with red eyes and huge teeth was growling at them from the garden next door.

Limpy tried to leap back, but couldn't move because Goliath was clinging to him.

'It's a reindeer,' squeaked Goliath. 'A vicious killer reindeer.'

The reindeer started to bark.

Limpy squinted at it through the fence. He tried to remember details about reindeer from the ad in the newspaper.

'I don't think it's a reindeer,' said Limpy. 'It hasn't got a red nose or tree branches growing out of its head. I think it's a dog.'

'I heard you call me a reindeer,' the dog growled at Goliath. 'You looking for a fight, wart-head?'

'Any time, dog-breath,' retorted Goliath.

Limpy saw that Goliath was flexing his poison glands. He grabbed Goliath before Goliath could squirt the dog through the fence.

'Don't,' pleaded Limpy. 'We're on a mission of peace and goodwill, remember?'

Goliath scowled at the dog and muttered things that had even less to do with peace and goodwill than the things the Christmas beetle had muttered at Limpy.

The dog growled even more angrily through the fence. Then it stood up.

Limpy gulped. He'd thought it was standing up before.

It was huge.

Limpy pulled Goliath away from the fence.

'That mongrel is history,' muttered Goliath,

glaring back at the growling monster dog. But Limpy was finding Goliath surprisingly easy to drag along the path towards Santa's workshop.

The front door was shut.

'Hmm,' said Limpy. 'We won't be able to do much Santa-helping if we can't find a way in.'

'I could get a stick and stab the door,' offered Goliath.

Limpy thanked him, but reminded him that from now on they'd be showing peace and goodwill to doors as well.

Goliath didn't look like he agreed.

Limpy explored the front verandah and found an open window.

'Come on,' he said to Goliath. 'We can get in through there.'

Goliath hesitated.

'What do we do once we're inside?' he said.

'Santa helper stuff,' said Limpy. 'You know, wrap presents, pack his lunchbox for the big trip, sort out his maps so he can find all the houses, that kind of thing.'

'And pack his cutlery?' said Goliath. 'In case he wants to stab other humans?'

Limpy didn't reply. He was too busy hopping up onto the window ledge and peering in.

The room was dark. For a moment Limpy thought it was empty. But when his eyes got used to the gloom he saw a shadowy figure sitting on a chair. It was Santa, his head in his hands, staring at the floor.

Limpy's warts prickled with concern.

He'd never seen a human look so miserable.

'What's the problem?' said Goliath, appearing at Limpy's side. 'Wishing you had that sharp stick?'

Limpy pointed at Santa, whose shoulders were so slumped that his beard was almost touching his knees.

'He probably had a rough day,' said Goliath. 'One of the reindeer probably pooed in his lunchbox.'

Limpy stared at Santa.

He had a feeling it was something even worse than that.

What could it be?

'We'll have to wait till he cheers up,' said Goliath. 'No point trying to knock his warts off with our helping skills while he's in that state.'

Limpy agreed.

As they hopped down onto the verandah, Limpy had a thought.

Santa's workshop seemed rather small, given that Santa would soon be loading up his sleigh with gifts for all the human children in the whole world.

Could that be why Santa was so miserable? Lack of storage space?

'Excuse me,' said a terse voice.

Limpy turned.

A spider was lowering itself towards them from a verandah post.

'Could you move?' said the spider. 'I'm trying to build a web here.'

'Sorry,' said Limpy. 'We'll get out of your way.'

'But only if you say please,' growled Goliath.

'Actually,' Limpy said to the spider, 'I wonder if you can help us. Do you happen to know where Santa stores his gifts?'

The spider looked confused, then annoyed.

'Santa?' said the spider. 'Gifts? Why are you asking me? I haven't got a clue. Um, a warehouse? Is this some kind of riddle? I am busy, you know.'

Sorry,' said Limpy. 'One other quick question. Any idea what time Santa starts work tomorrow?'

The spider glared at Limpy and waved its arms and legs impatiently.

'Do I look like an information website?' it said.

'Sorry to bother you,' said Limpy.

He turned to go. Out of the corner of his eye, he saw Goliath had grabbed the spider and was about to eat it.

'Hang on,' said the spider hastily. 'I've just remembered. It's Christmas Eve tomorrow. Biggest shopping day of the year. Santa will probably be working at the shopping mall, which opens at nine.'

'Thank you,' said Limpy. 'You've been a big help.'

He nudged Goliath, who gave the spider a last longing look and then put it back on the verandah post.

Limpy's warts tingled with excitement as he and Goliath hopped across Santa's front yard.

'This is perfect,' said Limpy. 'We can set off now, find the shopping mall, get inside before Santa arrives, and do lots of good helping things to prepare for Santa's biggest day of the year.'

'Can we get a pizza as well?' said Goliath. 'I bet North Pole pizzas are delicious.'

Before Limpy could reply, wart-chilling growls erupted from the other side of the garden fence.

Goliath hopped behind Limpy.

'Dog-breath,' he yelled at the vicious monster dog.

'Goliath,' said Limpy. 'Don't.'

Goliath glared at the fence. Then his expression changed.

'Hang on,' he said. 'I think that dog's inviting us over for pizza.'

'Listen more carefully,' said Limpy.

Goliath listened again to the growls.

'Yuck,' he muttered.

Limpy felt the same.

He hoped there weren't any other vicious monster dogs in this town who liked cane-toad pizzas.

Getting to the shopping mall wasn't easy.

This was partly because Limpy and Goliath didn't know exactly where to find it, and partly because they weren't exactly sure what a shopping mall was.

'Is that it?' said Goliath, peering into the hazy light from a row of street lamps.

'I don't think so,' said Limpy. 'I think that's a postbox.'

'What about that?' said Goliath.

'That's a house,' said Limpy.

They hopped on. The streets of the North Pole were full of houses and postboxes, but no shopping malls.

'I'm fed up with this,' said Goliath. 'Let's go into one of these houses and attack humans. They're all asleep in bed. We could stick mud up their noses and squash their hair with rocks.'

'No,' said Limpy firmly. 'We're Santa's helpers on a mission of peace and goodwill.'

'Spoilsport,' said Goliath. 'What if we never find this dumb mall?'

Limpy sighed.

He'd started to ask himself the same question.

'I don't think there is a shopping mall,' grumbled Goliath. 'I think it's just a story adults tell kids.'

After wandering around lost for the rest of the night and half the morning, Limpy and Goliath met a snail who knew where the shopping mall was.

'Behind you,' said the snail.

Limpy turned.

'Stack me,' he said.

They were in the shopping mall car park.

As they hopped closer, Limpy gazed up at the shopping mall. It was the biggest building he'd ever seen, even taller than a giant ant hill with a parents' retreat on the roof.

Limpy could see humans walking in and out of the mall, which meant it was already open, which meant that Santa was probably already there.

'Never mind,' said Limpy. 'We'll just have to be extra good helpers to make up for being late. But first we need to find Santa.'

'Easy,' said Goliath, squinting around the car park. 'Can you see any reindeer droppings?'

Limpy couldn't.

'Sorry,' said Goliath. 'I forgot. They do them in his lunchbox.'

'Did you say Santa?' piped up a voice.

It was a termite, munching on a wooden signpost.

'Galleria level, near the toy shop,' said the termite. 'Take the lift.'

'The lift?' said Limpy, alarmed. 'You mean the human lift?'

He'd heard elderly bush flies tell scary ancient legends about lifts. Big metal boxes full of humans. No windows.

'It's quite safe,' said the termite. 'I have lunch every day in the furniture store on the first floor. You'll be fine as long as you watch out for the feet. Humans hardly ever look down in lifts, only up.'

'Thanks,' said Limpy.

'This furniture store,' said Goliath to the termite. 'Do they sell pizzas?'

The termite was right.

Limpy and Goliath found a spot close to the lift wall, just inside the door, away from all the human feet.

None of the humans looked down.

'What a kind termite,' Limpy whispered to Goliath. 'I'm glad I persuaded you not to eat it.'

Goliath didn't look glad, just hungry.

'This galleria level,' he said. 'How will we know when we get there?'

Limpy wasn't sure.

Was galleria a number?

'Don't worry,' said a cockroach standing next to them. 'I know this mall like the back of my bottom.'

The lift stopped with a jolt and the lift doors opened.

'First floor,' announced the cockroach. 'Food scraps, grease blobs, dried flakes of human skin, bedding and sleepwear.'

'That's me,' said a bedbug, pushing past Limpy and Goliath.

Limpy winced as the bedbug disappeared with a faint pop under a human foot.

'Shopping,' sighed the cockroach. 'Gets harder every day.'

The doors closed and the lift moved upwards.

'Galleria level,' said the cockroach as the doors opened again. 'Expensive food scraps, low-fat grease blobs, moisturised flakes of human skin. Oh, and Santa Claus. Let the humans out first, please.'

Once the human feet had thundered out, Limpy thanked the cockroach and hopped out of the lift himself.

He glanced at Goliath to make sure he was safely out too.

'Goliath,' said Limpy. 'Spit the cockroach out.'

Goliath spat the cockroach out.

'Like I said,' mumbled the cockroach as he staggered back into the lift. 'Harder every day.'

Limpy gazed around.

The mall was huge and noisy and so bright it made his eyes go cloudy. He had to do lots of blinking before he could see clearly.

When he finally could, he nearly hopped back into the lift himself.

Herds of humans were roaming around, lumbering and jostling from shop to shop, weighed down by bags and packages.

Their faces were grim and determined.

This must be how humans look at Christmas, thought Limpy. When they're concentrating really hard on peace and goodwill.

'I smell pizza,' said Goliath excitedly.

He looked down. His face fell.

'No, hang on,' he said. 'It's just my feet.'

Then Limpy saw a red suit and black boots and a white beard.

Yes.

Santa was sitting on a big chair in a sort of cave. A human child was on his knee, and a long line of human adults and children were waiting their turn. Some of them were taking photos. Limpy knew about photos. Humans took them on picnics when other humans fell into swamps.

Limpy was pleased to see that Santa didn't look so sad today. His eyes were shining and he was saying, 'Ho, ho, ho', whatever that meant. The little human on his knee was laughing.

Santa's red suit looked brighter than Limpy remembered, and his boots seemed shinier and his beard whiter and fluffier.

Must be the strong lights in here, thought Limpy.

He took a deep breath.

This was it. The moment he and Goliath showed Santa they were his new very good helpers.

Just as Limpy was wondering exactly how to do that, he noticed something else different about Santa.

His hat.

It was a floppy red one that matched his suit, with a white fluffy bit on the end that matched his beard. Last night Santa hadn't been wearing a hat at all.

'Jumping gerbil gizzards,' said Goliath, elbowing Limpy in the rib warts. 'Look at that tree. Get a load of all the stuff growing on it.'

Limpy looked to where Goliath was pointing.

Right next to them, in a very big pot, was a very big tree the same shape as a pointy-headed beetle's pointy head. The tree was covered with blinking lights and dangling baubles and sparkling whatsits.

Limpy didn't have a clue what most of the baubles and whatsits were. He'd never been very good at nature studies. But there were other things on the tree he did recognise.

Santa dolls.

All wearing Santa hats.

Limpy stared at the hats, his warts tingling like warts often do when you have a really good idea.

Yes, he thought. Those are perfect for us.

'Oh well,' said Goliath gloomily. 'If there's no pizza, we'd better go and start helping Santa.'

'Not yet,' said Limpy. 'First we've got some tree climbing to do.'

Climbing the shopping mall Christmas tree wasn't easy.

The dangling whatsits kept whacking Limpy in the head, and every time the decorative lights blinked on they made Limpy's warts feel like bushfire-roasted gumnuts.

Also the tree was plastic.

'Unbelievable,' muttered Limpy as he struggled to cling on to the slippery plastic branches without being stabbed in the armpits by the prickly plastic tree-needles. 'Humans will be making plastic grass next.'

Climbing the tree was a struggle, but definitely worth doing. When Limpy reached a branch about halfway up, he saw that hanging from it was the very thing he was after.

A small Santa doll wearing a small Santa suit and, most importantly, a small Santa hat.

Limpy reached over and tried to pull the hat off

the Santa doll's head. At first it wouldn't budge. It seemed to be glued on. But when Limpy got closer and used his mouth, it came off.

Good old cane-toad dribble, thought Limpy. Dissolves almost anything if you use enough.

Limpy put the Santa hat on his own head.

Brilliant.

Now Santa'll know we're his new helpers, Limpy thought happily. All he's got to do is look at our professional headgear.

Limpy peered through the branches to see if Goliath had got himself a hat yet. It shouldn't be a problem, there were Santa dolls all over the tree.

'Goliath,' he called. 'Have you got one?'

'I've got heaps,' replied Goliath's distant voice.

'Where are you?' said Limpy.

'Just ducking up the top for a squiz around,' called Goliath. 'See if I can spot the pizza shop.'

Limpy squinted up through the branches.

There was Goliath, clambering upwards, a bundle of Santa hats in his mouth.

Limpy sighed.

'Come down,' he said. 'We've got to start our helping.'

'Won't be long,' called Goliath. 'Have a rest. Take the weight off your crook leg. Don't worry, I'll stay hidden.'

Limpy sighed again. When Goliath set his mind on something, all you could do was wait, unless you had a scorpion to prod him with.

Limpy waited.

While he was waiting he noticed a sock hanging from a nearby branch. Limpy knew about socks. Humans wore them on their feet. They were also an important part of Christmas. Most of the Christmas ads in the newspaper had at least one sock in them.

This sock had a pretty pattern of holly and candy canes, and was a nice green colour that reminded Limpy of Charm's eyes.

Suddenly Limpy felt very weary. It had been a long journey.

Maybe Goliath is right, thought Limpy. I'll have a bit of a rest before the hard helping work starts.

Limpy clambered into the sock, slipped his hat off and took the weight off his crook leg.

Ahhh.

That was better.

Except no sooner had he relaxed than someone was prodding the outside of the sock.

'That was quick, Goliath,' said Limpy as he stuck his head out.

But it wasn't Goliath.

It was a human child, her head close to Limpy's, her eyes wide as she stared at him.

She screamed.

Other humans started shouting and pointing at Limpy and some of them started screaming too.

Limpy was about to duck down inside the sock

again, when he noticed that other humans were pointing to the top of the tree.

Oh no.

Had something happened to Goliath?

Limpy looked anxiously upwards.

At the very top of the tree was an angel doll in a white dress. Limpy could tell it was a doll from the way it was staring straight ahead, completely unaware of who was sitting next to it.

Goliath.

He was wearing the angel's silver wings and halo, but his mouth was still stuffed with Santa hats, and he was peering around the mall with a hungry look.

Limpy saw that Goliath's attempt at staying hidden wasn't fooling the humans. Panic was spreading around the mall. Adults were grabbing children and running.

Limpy desperately tried to calm the humans.

'Don't be scared of us,' he shouted. 'We're just Santa's helpers. We want to be your friends. OK, we do have poison glands, but we hardly ever squirt them. I'm not planning to squirt anyone this whole Christmas holiday.'

It was hopeless. The humans couldn't understand a croak he was saying.

Plus, thought Limpy gloomily, when panic is in the air, who listens to a cane toad in a sock?

The panicking humans were banging into each other and knocking the tree as they lumbered past. The tree was wobbling.

It was more than wobbling, it was swaying.

'Goliath,' yelled Limpy. 'Hang on.'

Limpy held his breath inside the sock as the tree rocked and teetered and . . .

He felt himself falling and got ready for pain.

When it came, it felt like the world had crashed to pieces, and him too.

I'm dead, thought Limpy.

Then he realised that if he was thinking that, he couldn't be. The sock had saved him. Nestled him in its Christmas fluffiness and shown him more Christmas goodwill than any sock ever had before.

'Thank you,' croaked Limpy, and kissed the sock.

Then he remembered Goliath.

'Goliath,' he shouted, dragging himself out of the sock and looking around frantically.

The world hadn't crashed to pieces, but the tree definitely had.

Limpy scrambled through a tangle of twisted branches and dented baubles and smashed whatsits and crumpled Santa dolls and lights that were still blinking on and off, but with lots of smoke.

'Goliath,' yelled Limpy again.

'Ow,' said Goliath's voice, and there he was, sitting on a pile of festive rubble, pulling a piece of angel wing out of one of his nostrils.

'Come on,' said Limpy, starting to feel sick and giddy. 'We've got to get out of this smoke.'

'I dropped the hats,' said Goliath. 'But I think I've still got one or two.'

He frowned and started rummaging around inside his mouth.

'Hop for it,' yelled Limpy.

He grabbed Goliath, and together they scrambled through the smoke and broken branches, and finally collapsed in a cool puddle of liquid near the lift door.

'Ahhh,' said Goliath. 'That feels nice.'

It did, but all Limpy could think about was Santa.

Was he OK?

Limpy had a feeling that good helpers, wherever possible, did not crush their bosses under falling trees.

'Mmm,' said Goliath, tasting the puddle. 'Melted ice-cream.'

Limpy was only half-listening.

Most of the humans in the mall had disappeared, but a few were still running around. One of them, Limpy now saw with relief, was Santa. He looked fine. He was hurrying towards some mechanical stairs that were climbing down by themselves.

Limpy stared.

It wasn't the mechanical stairs that made his mouth fall open.

Santa was pulling his beard off as he ran. And underneath, Limpy saw in amazement, was a teenager.

'Stack me,' said Limpy. 'That's not the real Santa.'

'I think this is choc chip,' said Goliath, licking his lips. 'Or vanilla with ticks in it.'

Limpy stared through the billowing smoke as the teenage Santa disappeared down the mechanical stairs.

He didn't understand.

The real Santa was here in town. They'd ridden in the back of his ute. So why was the shopping mall using a fake Santa?

Limpy didn't have time to work it out right now. Flames were flickering among the Christmas tree branches. Melted plastic was creeping towards him and Goliath.

'Come on,' said Limpy. 'We've got to get out of here.'

'One more lick,' said Goliath, his tongue darting back into the puddle.

At that moment burning plastic dribbled into the ice-cream, making it sizzle. Goliath hastily pulled his tongue away.

'OK,' he said to Limpy. 'I've had enough.'

But Limpy was only half-listening again. Doors were crashing open on the other side of the mall. Humans were running in.

Limpy gawked.

The humans were all wearing black boots. And red jackets and pants.

A gang of Santas?

With hoses and axes and fire extinguishers?

Limpy realised who they were.

'That's weird,' he said. 'Why are those firefighters all dressed like Santa?'

As Limpy and Goliath watched the firefighters putting out the burning Christmas tree, Limpy started to have an uncomfortable feeling deep in his guts.

'Don't be dopey,' muttered Goliath. 'Firefighters just wear the same colour as Santa, that's all. If they were dressed up as him they'd all have beards.'

Limpy nodded. Goliath was right. No beards.

Except for one of them.

Limpy stared.

One of the firefighters, the most elderly, who was giving orders to the others, had a white beard. A very familiar white beard.

Oh no, thought Limpy.

Now he was feeling very sick and giddy even though the smoke had stopped.

'Goliath,' he said. 'I think I've made a terrible mistake.'

Limpy decided that when hundreds of angry human shoppers and two cane toads are evacuated into a shopping mall car park on Christmas Eve, the cane toads, if they've got any sense, hide under a parked car.

'Quick,' he said to Goliath. 'Hide under this parked car.'

Goliath didn't try to argue. He was too busy complaining.

'How could you?' he said. 'How could you think a firefighter was Santa? Just because their clothes are similar. And their beards. And their utes. And their dedication to peace and goodwill. How could you?'

Limpy sighed as they crouched under the car.

'I'm sorry, Goliath,' he said. 'I made a mistake.'

'A firefighter,' said Goliath, 'is not Santa.'

Limpy reminded himself how Goliath took a while to get used to things. Like the time he discovered that swamp slugs didn't have kidneys, which were his favourite snack. For days afterwards he wandered around the swamp saying, 'I can't believe it'.

'You thought a firefighter was Santa,' said Goliath. 'I can't believe it.'

Limpy peered out from under the car, trying to see where the firefighters were. Perhaps he hadn't made a mistake after all. Perhaps the firefighter with the beard was actually Santa doing a bit of volunteer fire fighting.

Silly idea, forget it.

'This isn't even the North Pole,' muttered Goliath. 'Santa doesn't even live here.'

Limpy felt his warts starting to sag with disappointment and despair.

No, he thought, I'm not going to let that happen.

He perked his warts up.

OK, he said to himself. There must be other ways we can meet Santa and join his team and win the hearts of humans everywhere. Our quest isn't a total failure yet.

Goliath had his head in his hands.

'Our quest is a total failure,' he wailed.

Limpy struggled to keep his warts perked.

'Goliath,' he said. 'Do you remember when you found that nest of yummy stink-grubs high up in that tree. And you couldn't knock them down, not even with a very long stick. You didn't give up, did you?'

'Yes I did,' said Goliath. 'I ate the stick.'

Limpy sighed and wished he'd thought of a better example.

'Goliath,' he said. 'Have you still got those Santa hats?'

Goliath nodded and held up two soggy Santa hats. Limpy took one and put it on. Goliath put the other one on.

'Brilliant,' said Limpy. 'My spirits are up already.'

'Same here,' said Goliath. 'Now all I need to do is get my strength up.'

Before Limpy could stop him, Goliath hopped over to the people-mover parked next to them and started climbing up the side.

Limpy saw what was in the people-mover.

People.

In the drivers seat was a human lady fiddling with the CD player. In the back seats were human children busy with brightly coloured paper and sticky tape, wrapping presents.

Except for one child, who was eating pizza.

'Goliath,' yelled Limpy. 'Come back.'

The rear window was partly open, and Goliath was already squeezing himself through the gap.

The busy humans hadn't noticed.

Limpy didn't have any choice.

He followed.

Limpy decided that when two cane toads squeeze themselves into a human people-mover uninvited, and the people-mover suddenly drives off, the cane toads, if they've got any sense, hide on the floor in the back under some crumpled Christmas wrapping paper.

Limpy huddled under the wrapping paper, hoping desperately that Goliath had the sense to do the same. With Goliath you could never be sure.

'Goliath,' whispered Limpy. 'Are you OK?'

No reply.

Limpy didn't panic. It was noisy in the people-mover with the throbbing engine and the rumbling wheels and the chattering humans. Goliath probably couldn't hear him.

Just be patient, Limpy told himself. The people-mover will stop soon and the humans will get out and then we can go back to our quest. Just as long as Goliath hasn't tried to take their pizza.

Limpy knew what human children could do when somebody tried to take their pizza.

It wasn't pretty.

Finally the people-mover stopped and Limpy heard the doors opening.

He lay very still under the wrapping paper until the human voices drifted away, then he wriggled out and looked around.

No Goliath.

Just a human baby in a human baby seat, staring fiercely at Limpy.

Limpy gulped.

He knew human babies were very strong. He'd

seen them on picnics, tearing sandwiches and fluffy toys apart with their bare hands. This baby looked pretty annoyed at being left in the people-mover while its family took the shopping into the house.

Limpy gulped again.

If the baby leapt at him and got its hands round his neck . . .

Then he saw with relief that the baby was strapped into the seat. But he also noticed something else, something that didn't make him feel quite so relieved.

The baby was holding a Christmas present. And from inside the parcel was coming the muffled sound of a familiar indignant voice.

'Limpy. Get me out of here.'

Limpy stared at the parcel.

'Goliath,' he said. 'Is that you?'

'Yes,' said Goliath's voice. 'Help. I don't want to be a Christmas present.'

Limpy leapt into action.

He started pulling funny faces and blowing raspberries with his skin pores and doing silly things with his bottom. Everything that always made Goliath clap his hands with delight.

It worked.

The baby clapped its hands with delight. The Christmas present tumbled onto the floor.

'Ow,' groaned the parcel. 'Limpy. Help. You don't have to wait till Christmas Day. Unwrap me now.'

Limpy tore at the paper. Gradually, as he ripped the layers off, Goliath appeared, still wearing his Santa hat, lying squashed against a plastic space warrier with a big sword.

Goliath struggled out of the last shreds of paper and sticky tape, and glared at the plastic warrier.

'Thanks for not helping me escape,' he said bitterly. 'And next time, watch where you're pointing that sword.'

The human baby was looking at Goliath and chuckling.

Goliath glared at the baby.

'Come on,' said Limpy to Goliath. 'Let's get out of here before the other humans come back.'

'That kid's lucky I haven't got time to arm wrestle it,' muttered Goliath, giving the baby a last stare.

They hopped out of the half-open door and hurried away from the people-mover as fast as they could.

Limpy looked around to see where they were.

A street, full of houses.

It was dusk and lights were coming on.

Limpy's first thought was to stay away from the lights. Until he saw some lights he wanted to get much closer to.

Further down the street, a house was covered in sparkling Christmas lights. And on the roof, brightest of all, made from millions of the tiny lights, was a huge twinkling picture of Santa and his sleigh.

'Galloping gumnuts,' gasped Goliath.

Limpy had to agree.

'Stack me,' he said. 'Santa's landing pad.'

'Santa's what?' said Goliath.

'When Santa's approaching in the night sky,' explained Limpy, 'these lights help guide him in for a landing. Which is really good for us, because we get to meet him after all.'

'We do?' said Goliath. 'How?'

'Easy,' said Limpy. 'We just climb up on the roof and wait.'

'Santa's not coming,' said Goliath gloomily for the millionth time.

Limpy thought about pushing Goliath off the roof, but only for a moment. Then he remembered how much he loved Goliath, and went back to staring up at the night sky.

Waiting.

Hoping.

There were plenty of stars and planets and fireflies, but nothing that looked like a sleigh, not even in the distance. The only Santa in sight was the one traced out in sparkling lights around Limpy and Goliath on the roof.

'This is the worst Christmas Eve I've ever had,' moaned Goliath.

Limpy sighed.

They'd been waiting most of the night. Where was Santa? It didn't seem fair after all the effort they'd put into reaching the landing pad.

Climbing up onto the roof of a human house was hard enough, specially with a crook leg. It was even harder when you were lugging a sock full of presents you'd collected to add to Santa's supply and show what a good helper you were.

'Our quest is a total failure,' moaned Goliath.

Limpy struggled to keep his warts from drooping.

'I'm not gunna get any pizza from Santa,' said Goliath, 'so it's a total failure.' He took off his Santa hat and started chewing it mournfully. 'We'll be dead of old age and hunger before he arrives.'

Limpy pulled his own Santa hat firmly onto his head and made a decision.

'OK,' he said. 'Let's start without him.'

Goliath gave Limpy a doubtful look.

'Start?' he said. 'Refuelling the reindeer?'

'No,' said Limpy. 'Delivering gifts to humans.'

Goliath stared.

'Without Santa?' he said.

'Why not?' said Limpy. 'That's why we're here, isn't it? To share Christmas peace and goodwill with humans so they'll want to be our friends.'

Goliath gave another doubtful look, this time at the two bulging Christmas socks.

'It's OK,' said Limpy. 'We're the ones who borrowed these socks from a human washing line. We're the ones who spent ages collecting all the gifts. We're allowed to hand them out.'

Now Goliath was looking confused.

'I thought these gifts were for us,' he said. 'To give each other for Christmas.'

Limpy stared at Goliath. He suddenly had a strong urge to give Goliath a hug.

Stack me, he thought. This must be what Christmas peace and goodwill is all about. One moment you want to push your cousin off a roof for being so annoying, and the next you wouldn't swap him for the biggest slug sausage in the world.

Limpy heaved his sock onto his shoulder.

'Come on,' he said to Goliath. 'Put your hat on, grab your sock and let's get down that chimney.'

'This chimney's very slimy and greasy,' said Goliath. 'I like it.'

In the darkness Limpy couldn't see what Goliath was doing, but he could hear sounds of licking and lip-smacking.

'Are all chimneys this yummy?' said Goliath.

'It's not actually a chimney,' said Limpy. 'Human houses don't have chimneys here in the tropics. The Christmas beetle reckons that round here, Santa usually comes in through the kitchen fan exhaust pipe.'

'Yum,' said Goliath. 'Clever Santa.'

They squeezed past some greasy plastic fan blades. Limpy hoped they were almost at the end of the exhaust pipe. His sock was starting to feel very heavy.

Up ahead he could see faint light coming in

through some sort of round door with holes in it.

Hope we can open that, thought Limpy. I'm sure we can, or else how would Santa get in?

'Ow,' said Limpy as he landed on the kitchen bench with a thud.

The drop was further than it looked.

'You OK?' said Goliath next to him.

'Just a bit dazed,' said Limpy, pulling his Santa hat back on.

'I know how you feel,' said Goliath. 'My foot went really dazed when I kicked that round door out.'

Luckily the kitchen bench was next to a window, so the benchtop was in bright moonlight and Limpy found their gift-filled socks without any trouble.

The trouble started when he turned back to Goliath.

'What's that you've got?' said Limpy anxiously.

Goliath was fiddling with something on the benchtop. It was plastic and it had a windscreen.

'I think it's a mobile phone,' said Goliath. 'It's a bit like the one I almost swallowed once at a human camp site. I've almost got it switched on.'

'Leave it,' begged Limpy. 'If it rings, it'll wake up the humans.'

'But we could give Santa a call,' said Goliath. 'Let him know things are going OK here. Ask him how he usually gets out of a house when the kitchen fan exhaust pipe is too high up to hop back into.'

'Goliath,' said Limpy, exasperated.

'You're right,' said Goliath, sagging. 'We haven't got his number.'

'It'll be OK,' said Limpy, giving his cousin a pat on the warts. 'We'll find a way out. But first we've got work to do.'

He pushed one of the socks towards Goliath and heaved the other one onto his shoulder.

Then he stopped and stared.

At the other end of the benchtop, two big fluffy balls had suddenly appeared, one white and one grey. They looked like they were from two gigantic Santa hats.

But Limpy realised they weren't.

Santa-hat fluffy bits didn't have eyes. Or, when they yawned, very sharp-looking teeth.

'What do you think you're doing?' said one of the big fluffy balls. 'And why are you carrying those silly socks?'

'Just our luck,' muttered Goliath. 'Cats. I don't like cats. They always say really hurtful things and start fights.'

Limpy took a step towards the cats and tried to look friendly and full of Christmas peace and goodwill.

'Season's greetings,' he said. 'We're Santa's helpers. We've come bearing gifts for the humans of the house. And the pets too, of course.'

'What sort of gifts?' said the white cat.

'Lots of things,' said Limpy, rummaging around in his sock. 'Some lovely dead ants, and some gumnuts, and some gravel that really helps your digestion when you get bunged up, and . . .'

He decided to show them, and tipped the contents of his sock out onto the benchtop.

The cats looked at everything. Limpy could see they weren't impressed.

He nudged Goliath, who tipped out his sock too.

'We've got some dried beetle wings,' said Limpy. 'They're very beautiful when you hold them up in the moonlight.'

He saw that the contents of Goliath's sock was mostly dried mud.

'Where are the beetle wings?' he whispered to Goliath.

'Um,' said Goliath. 'I ate them.'

Limpy turned back to the cats, who were trying not to snigger. He pushed the pile of gifts towards them.

'Happy Christmas,' he said, still trying to look friendly and full of peace and goodwill.

'Very kind,' said the grey cat. 'But tragically pathetic.'

'Ungrateful fluff-ball,' muttered Goliath. 'What you need is an arm wrestle.'

'Come with us,' said the white cat to Limpy and Goliath. 'There's something you should see.'

As Limpy followed the cats into the lounge room, he could hear the distant sounds of human snoring from the other end of the house.

That was a relief at least.

The humans were safely asleep.

Then the white cat prodded a lamp switch with its paw, and Limpy saw something that didn't make him feel very relieved at all.

In the centre of the room was a Christmas tree. It was much smaller than the one in the shopping mall, but around it, almost blocking it from view, were piles of presents.

Big presents, wrapped in gold and silver paper.

Loads of them.

'Leaping lizard legs,' said Goliath. 'That's a lot of pizzas.'

'Musical cat bowl,' said the white cat, pointing to one of the shiny boxes. 'I saw our owners wrapping it.'

'Brushed-nylon leopard-skin sleeping pod,' said the grey cat, pointing to another wrapped box. 'With my initials on it.'

'And,' said the white cat, 'we're both getting mechanical mice that are also MP3 players.'

'Plus,' said the grey cat, 'there are the things our owners are giving each other. Coffee-making machine, blu-ray video recorder, his and hers imported tracksuits, automatic lint-remover . . .'

'They couldn't get the lint-remover,' said the white cat. 'Sold out, remember?'

'Oh yes, that's right,' said the grey cat. 'They were really disappointed.'

And they weren't the only ones.

Limpy caught sight of his reflection in the side of a big silver-wrapped box. He saw how much his warts were drooping. And his bottom lip as well.

He knew why.

The cats were right.

Compared to these gifts, dead ants and gravel did seem a bit tragically pathetic. Limpy couldn't imagine them winning the friendship of many humans, not even ones who were bunged up.

'Thank you,' Limpy said to the cats. 'You've been very kind.'

'No they haven't,' hissed Goliath, glaring at the cats. 'They've been very pooey.'

But Limpy felt grateful to the cats. Because now he knew exactly what he and Goliath had to do.

Limpy hopped out through the cat door into a moonlit backyard.

While he waited for Goliath to follow, he asked himself a question.

How can two cane toads, a muscly one and one with a crook leg, get urgent supplies of the sort of presents humans like? Not dumb old dead flies and gumnuts. Things you plug in.

Limpy knew there had to be an answer.

He turned to see if Goliath had any suggestions.

Goliath was stuck in the cat door. This was mostly because of the bulging Christmas sock he was trying to drag through with him.

Limpy sighed and went to help. Through the glass he could see that the cats were both pushing Goliath from behind.

'Ow,' complained Goliath. 'Careful with those claws.'

Limpy grabbed a big wart and pulled, and finally Goliath popped out.

So did his sock.

'Sorry,' Goliath said to Limpy. 'But no way was I gunna leave perfectly good dead flies and gravel for those ungrateful fluff-balls.'

He turned and poked his tongue out at the smirking cats.

'Ignore them,' said Limpy. 'We've got more important things to think about.'

'Getting a bigger cat door?' said Goliath.

Limpy shook his head.

'Looks like Santa is seriously delayed,' he said, 'so we need to get hold of some bigger and better human gifts ourselves.'

Goliath looked doubtful.

'Better gifts?' he said. 'You mean better than gravel?'

Limpy only half-heard, because at that moment he noticed a dark shape at the end of the backyard.

He stared at it.

It was the answer to their problem.

'Look at that,' said Limpy, pointing. 'Do you know what that is?'

Goliath peered at the shape.

'No,' he said. 'I don't.'

'It's a shed,' said Limpy.

'A what?' said Goliath.

'A shed,' repeated Limpy, more loudly in case Goliath was having hearing problems. Sometimes when Goliath was eating, bits of food tried to escape through his ears.

'A shed?' said Goliath.

'I've seen ads for sheds in newspapers,' said Limpy. 'Sheds have tools in them. Tools that are good for making things.'

'What sort of things?' said Goliath.

'All sorts of things,' said Limpy. 'Automatic lint-removers, for example.'

There were quite a few tools in the shed.

Limpy didn't have a clue what most of them were, and Goliath clearly didn't either. But that didn't stop Goliath pulling them down from their hooks and cutting his hand on a couple of them.

'Ow,' said Goliath. 'That one's sharp. Ow, so's that one.'

While Goliath sucked his fingers, Limpy realised they had another problem.

'I'm not completely sure,' he said, 'what a lint-remover is.'

'Me neither,' said Goliath. 'But it can't be hard to work out. Lint's like hair and fluff and wispy bits, right? The stuff we eat when we haven't got salad?'

'The stuff you eat,' said Limpy.

'Right,' said Goliath. 'So a lint-remover must be something that removes it.'

Limpy couldn't argue with that.

'What I'm not sure about,' he said to Goliath, 'is what a lint-remover actually removes lint from.'

Goliath frowned.

'Places it builds up on humans?' he said. 'Like their belly buttons?'

‘Could be,’ said Limpy. ‘Or maybe their clothes. They’re always brushing things off their clothes on picnics. Scorpions and things like that.’

‘OK,’ said Goliath. ‘So what we have to build is a gift that automatically removes lint from human clothes, and removes scorpions as well.’

Limpy nodded doubtfully.

Suddenly he wasn’t feeling quite so confident. He’d never used human tools in his life. He wasn’t even that experienced with sharp sticks.

‘OK,’ said Goliath enthusiastically, rubbing his hands together and looking around the shed in the moonlight. ‘Leave it to me.’

Limpy was impressed.

The floor of the shed was littered with bits of bent wire that Goliath had managed to make even more bent, and lengths of knotted string that Goliath had tied even more knots in, and lumps of wood with Goliath’s teethmarks on them.

Goliath might not be tidiest inventor in the world, thought Limpy, but he certainly doesn’t give up easily.

‘Limpy,’ said Goliath. ‘Could you pass me that screwdriver please?’

Limpy passed him the screwdriver.

Goliath opened his mouth, jammed the sharp end down his throat and jiggled it around.

‘That’s better,’ he said, pulling it out and swallowing. ‘Some gravel got stuck.’

Goliath turned back to his invention.

'Looking good,' he said. 'All I've got to do now is make it remove lint.'

Limpy had to admit that after all the failed experiments with the wire and the string and the wood, it had been a clever idea of Goliath's to adapt a machine that was already in the shed.

True, the only adapting Goliath had done so far was pulling the cover off and staring at the machine for a long time, but Limpy could see Goliath was coming to a decision.

'Those bits there,' said Goliath, pointing to some flat metal bits. 'Those are the bits that will remove the lint.'

He leaned over and dribbled onto the flat metal bits.

'I'm doing this,' he said, 'to make them what we inventors call sticky.'

'Brilliant,' said Limpy.

He was really enjoying Goliath being in charge for a change. It was a big relief, not having to try to make friends with the whole human race all on your own.

But he did have one little concern.

'Those flat metal bits look sharp,' said Limpy.

'Yeah,' said Goliath. 'They have to be.'

Limpy frowned.

That did look like it might be a problem. But before he could say anything, another voice said it for him.

'Big problem, that.'

Limpy saw the voice belonged to a woodworm who had crawled out of a floorboard.

'Your problem,' said the woodworm, 'is that when humans start that lawnmower up and try to use it to remove lint from their clothes, it'll slice them to bits and kill them.'

'So?' said Goliath.

Limpy stared at the machine.

'Goliath,' he said quietly, struggling not to explode. 'We're on a mission of peace and goodwill. To make friends with humans. Not give them a present that's going to kill them.'

Goliath was staring sulkily at the floor.

'It might not kill all of them,' he muttered. 'Not if they're careful.'

A beautiful shaft of dawn sunlight came in through the shed window. It wasn't enough to stop Limpy's shoulders drooping wearily.

'It's morning,' said the woodworm. 'Christmas morning. Happy Christmas.'

'Happy Christmas,' muttered Goliath.

Limpy didn't say anything.

It wasn't feeling like a very happy Christmas at all.

The early morning sun threw dark shadows down the street.

Two of the shadows hopped slowly and wearily away from a house with a shed in its backyard.

The small hopping shadow gave a big sigh.

The large hopping shadow didn't reply. Just stuck its hand into a shadow sock, pulled out some shadow gravel and ate it.

As Limpy hopped, he stared at his dark bobbing self on the footpath in front of him.

Experienced shadow experts, he thought, like owls or glow-worms, would probably be thinking that just because my shoulders are sagging and my warts are drooping, I'm a cane toad who's given up on a really important mission.

Well they'd be wrong.

Limpy remembered what Dad always said.

If at first you don't succeed, try, try again.

That's three tries all together, thought Limpy.

Which means we've still got one try to go.

He straightened his shoulders and perked up his warts.

'Happy Christmas,' he said to Goliath.

Goliath crunched some gravel with a droopy mouth.

'What's happy about it?' he said. 'We didn't even meet Santa.'

'I know,' said Limpy. 'That was bad luck. He must have come while we were in the shed. But it doesn't matter. Even without Santa, we can still make this mission a success.'

Goliath gave Limpy the sort of look you give a dung beetle who's forgotten what dung is.

'It's Christmas morning,' continued Limpy. 'Soon humans everywhere will be waking up full of Christmas cheer. Their warts will be tingling with it. Or their pimples if they haven't got warts.'

'What's your point?' said Goliath.

'This is the one day of the year all humans are full of peace and goodwill,' said Limpy. 'It's the perfect day for us to make friends with them. We mustn't waste it.'

Goliath reached into his sock, put a dead fly into his mouth and sucked mournfully.

'We left our Santa hats in the shed,' he said. 'The cats'll probably use them to store kitty litter in. So what are we gunna do? Stick twigs in our heads and pretend to be reindeer?'

Limpy grinned.

He had a better idea than that.

'There's more to Christmas than hats,' he said. 'I think it's time to try something different. What do humans give each other at Christmas, apart from presents?'

Goliath had a think.

'Colds?' he said.

'Christmas cards,' said Limpy.

Limpy had never made a Christmas card before. He'd seen silverfish giving them to each other, or bits of them, and he knew how they worked and what they were made of. So finding a pizza box in a rubbish bin was a big stroke of luck. Specially with half a pizza in it.

'Yay,' yelled Goliath, grabbing the box. 'I'm having a happy Christmas after all.'

'Don't eat the pizza,' said Limpy.

'Why not?' said Goliath. 'Santa probably left it for me.'

Limpy showed Goliath why.

He tore the bottom off the box and folded it in half to make a card. Then he lifted the cheese off the pizza and dipped his finger into the tomato paste and drew a happy Christmas scene on the front of the card.

'What is it?' said Goliath, staring at the drawing.

'Cane toads and humans,' said Limpy. 'Sharing a happy and friendly Christmas Day together.'

'Why are they covered in tomato paste?' said Goliath.

'They're making pizzas,' said Limpy.

He let Goliath do the inside of the card.

They couldn't do a message because of the language problem, so Goliath drew humans and cane toads on a mud slide together.

'Those humans,' said Limpy suspiciously. 'They've all got sticks poking out of their heads. Are they pretending to be reindeer?'

He could tell from Goliath's guilty expression they weren't. So he made Goliath erase all the sticks. Goliath didn't mind that much because he got to do it with his tongue.

The first human Limpy chose to give the Christmas card to was a man in a dressing gown. He was pegging underwear on a clothes line in a backyard.

'Look at those lovely colourful pegs,' said Limpy. 'I bet he got them for Christmas and couldn't wait to try them out.'

Goliath swallowed the last bit of pizza and glowered at the pegs.

'They wouldn't be lovely clamped to a wart,' he said.

Limpy hopped up onto the back fence and started waving to the man.

'Happy Christmas,' he shouted.

He held the card up so the man could see it.

The man didn't even look round.

'I knew this wouldn't work,' grunted Goliath, hopping onto the fence next to Limpy. 'The dopey mongrel can't understand a croak you're saying.'

'He will when he sees the card,' said Limpy. 'You try. You've got a louder voice.'

'Happy Christmas,' croaked Goliath, scowling at the man.

'Wave as well,' said Limpy.

Goliath waved his fists.

After a lot more waving and yelling, the man finally turned round.

Limpy held the card out and made his warts glow with Christmas cheer. He waited for the surprised expression on the man's face to change into a smile of peace and goodwill.

It didn't. It changed into a glare of hatred.

A peg hurtled past Limpy's head. And another.

'I don't think this mongrel likes Christmas cards,' said Goliath, ducking.

'It's us he doesn't like,' said Limpy sadly. 'Come on, hop for it.'

They jumped down from the fence and hurried along the street and hid in a stormwater drain.

'Can I eat the card now?' said Goliath.

'No,' said Limpy. 'We'll try again with another human in a while. It's probably a bit early for peace and goodwill right now. Humans are always a bit grumpy first thing in the morning.'

Goliath insisted on choosing the next human.

'That one,' he said, pointing to a woman crouched by her car at the side of the street.

She was changing a flat tyre.

'Are you sure?' said Limpy doubtfully.

'Leave her to me,' said Goliath. 'It's not too early any more. She's had time for coffee and turkey pizza. I bet she got that hydraulic jack for Christmas and gave herself a puncture just so she could use it.'

Limpy wasn't sure about that.

The woman looked very red in the face, and was muttering things Limpy suspected were rude.

Before Limpy could stop him, Goliath put his sock down, grabbed the card and hopped over to the woman.

'Happy Christmas,' he croaked loudly.

The woman looked at him.

Then, to Limpy's horror, she grabbed the metal stick she'd been using to try to get the tyre off the wheel, and used it to try to get Goliath's head off his body.

Luckily her first lunge missed.

Goliath hopped backwards.

'Hey,' he said indignantly to the woman. 'If you don't like your Christmas present, don't blame me. I'm not Santa. I'm not even Santa's helper. I've never even met the bloke.'

The woman swung at Goliath's head again.

'Goliath,' yelled Limpy. 'This way.'

They hopped for it and hid in another stormwater drain.

'This is a dopey idea,' growled Goliath. 'Humans

have always hated us and they'll never be friends with us.'

'They will,' said Limpy. 'I'm sure they will. We just have to find the right human to start the whole thing off. Come on, let's give it one more go.'

They found a human who seemed perfect.

He looked well-rested, well-fed and, best of all, he was wearing a Santa hat with his shorts and thongs so he was clearly full of Christmas cheer and goodwill. Plus the chainsaw he was trimming his hedge with was gleaming and new, so Limpy and Goliath agreed he must be really happy.

'When we give him the card,' said Goliath hopefully, 'do you think he'll let us have a go of the chainsaw?'

'First things first,' said Limpy.

He hopped close to the human's feet. He didn't bother shouting because of the noise of the chainsaw, just held the card out.

The human didn't notice.

Goliath did bother shouting. Also he grabbed a stick and started bashing it against a can of chainsaw fuel.

'Hey, pay attention, you wartless wonder,' roared Goliath. 'We're wishing you a happy Christmas.'

The human still didn't pay attention. Limpy could see he didn't even know they were there.

But all that suddenly changed around the time Goliath stopped bashing the fuel can and started bashing the human's ankle.

'Hop for it,' screamed Limpy as the chainsaw swung down towards them in a cloud of smoke and human curses.

They hopped for it, through the hedge and down the street.

Limpy looked around desperately for another stormwater drain. For ages he couldn't see one. Just a teenager trying to run them over with his new trail bike, then a woman trying to stab them with her new cutlery set, then a man trying to tie them up with his new tie, then a toddler trying to colour them in with her new textas, then a pensioner trying to bash them with his new walking frame.

Even when Limpy finally did find another stormwater drain, and he and Goliath flopped exhausted into it, a gang of crayfish tried to put Limpy in one of their new plastic supermarket bags they reckoned Santa had sent them in the last downpour.

Goliath chased the crayfish away.

Limpy slumped against the wall of the drain. He tried to perk his warts up, but it was no good.

Goliath's right, he thought miserably. Humans have always hated cane toads and they always will. And no amount of Christmas or presents or cards or Santa will ever change that. Ever. Our mission is a total failure.

Limpy felt sick with disappointment.

'I'm sorry, Goliath,' he said. 'Let's go home. I was wrong. There's no such thing as Christmas peace and goodwill. That Christmas beetle must have made it all up.'

Goliath was slumped as well, hugging his sock and chewing.

'I bet he's not even a real Christmas beetle,' said Goliath bitterly through a mouthful of Christmas card. 'I bet he's just a swamp beetle in a hat.'

Limpy and Goliath hopped wearily along the street towards the firefighter's house, trying to stay out of the searing Christmas Day sun as much as possible.

'I'm hot,' croaked Goliath, shifting his sock from one shoulder to the other.

Limpy felt the same.

And exhausted and miserable.

He tried to cheer Goliath up.

'At least we found our way back,' said Limpy. 'Thanks to that kind frog in the drain giving us directions. That was lucky, him knowing the video shop on the corner.'

It didn't work.

Goliath just scowled and muttered something about how he'd rather have eaten the frog.

Limpy gave up.

He knew exactly how Goliath felt.

When you've just failed in the most important quest of your life, who wants to be cheered up?

'Let's not hang around,' said Limpy as they hopped closer to the house. 'Let's just grab Uncle Vasco from the ute and head home.'

Goliath grunted in agreement.

As they got closer to the firefighter's house, Limpy couldn't look at it. Just the thought of it made his warts ache with disappointment.

'Santa's workshop,' said Goliath scornfully. 'Were we dopey or what? If that was Santa's workshop, the TV aerial wouldn't be on the roof, it'd be on a reindeer.'

'You weren't dopey,' said Limpy, staring at the footpath. 'I was.'

Goliath thought about this.

'Fair enough,' he said.

Then he stopped.

'Oh poop,' he grunted.

Limpy looked up. And saw they were out the front of the house. He also saw what Goliath was staring at. Not the wonky TV aerial on the roof. The empty space at the kerb.

The ute was gone.

'Oh no,' wailed Goliath. 'Uncle Vasco's been kidnapped.'

Limpy peered up and down the street. No sign of the ute. Plus it wasn't in the driveway or down the side of the house. And there was no garage, so it couldn't be hiding.

'A human's stolen our uncle,' wailed Goliath.

Limpy realised what must have happened.

'Calm down,' he said to Goliath. 'I bet the firefighter has just gone to his family or friends for Christmas lunch. You know how maggots are always getting together for family meals? Well humans are the same. He'll be back later.'

'He'd better be,' growled Goliath. 'Or I'm gunna set fire to his house. And his firefighter's hat.'

'Come on,' said Limpy. 'We haven't slept for ages. Let's have a snooze in the shade while we wait.'

He led Goliath into the front yard.

They flopped down in the shade of some bushes, well away from the fence and the big scary dog.

Except, thought Limpy sleepily as he closed his eyes, it does seem very quiet next door. The big scary dog must be off having Christmas lunch too.

Limpy didn't sleep exactly, just dozed.

There was too much to worry about.

How to get home, mostly.

Stormwater drains were the safest method of travel. But the frog who'd given them directions had also given them the bad news.

The drains stopped at the edge of town.

Which meant there was only one way back to the swamp. A long and dangerous hop along the highway. Carrying Uncle Vasco. Dodging cars driven by humans with absolutely no Christmas peace and goodwill in their hearts.

'Happy Christmas,' roared an angry voice.

Limpy's eyes snapped open.

For a horrible moment he thought the dog next door had decided to have him and Goliath for its Christmas lunch.

But there was no sign of the dog. And Goliath wasn't flopped on the grass any more. Only his sock was.

'Happy Christmas and a pooey new year, you mongrels,' roared the voice.

Limpy realised who the voice belonged to.

He jumped up frantically and peered around. There was Goliath, squatting in the middle of the road, waving a stick angrily at what Limpy could now see was an approaching vehicle.

'Goliath,' shouted Limpy. 'Don't do it. Get off the road. Please.'

He hurried towards Goliath as fast as he could.

'Don't try to stop me,' said Goliath. 'Those mongrel humans had their chance. But they don't want to be friends, they just want to squash us flat and kidnap our uncles. Well this is showdown time. I'm an angry cane toad and I've got a stick.'

Limpy grabbed Goliath's big arm and tried to drag him off the road. But as usual when Goliath was angry and hysterical, he was also too heavy.

The vehicle coming towards them was very close now. Too close for them to get away.

Suddenly Limpy knew this was it.

A sad end to a sad Christmas.

He hugged Goliath and whispered goodbye to Mum and Dad and Charm and stared bravely at the very last vehicle he would ever see.

And recognised it.

The ute.

There behind the steering wheel was the fire-fighter, his beard white and bushy as ever.

Thank swamp, thought Limpy. We're saved. He'll swerve and miss us again.

Then Limpy had a horrible thought.

What if he doesn't?

What if he only swerved last time because he coughed or sneezed or nodded off?

What if he's a miserable grump who doesn't have a flicker of peace and goodwill in any of his internal organs or body cavities?

Just another human who hates cane toads?

'Eat wood, you mongrel,' Goliath yelled at the ute, brandishing his stick.

But no wood was eaten.

Limpy saw the firefighter's eyes widen with alarm as he desperately turned the steering wheel.

The ute swerved across the road.

It thumped into the kerb and stopped with two wheels up on the footpath.

'Chicken,' yelled Goliath.

Limpy was too weak with relief to speak to Goliath about his manners.

The firefighter, who was squinting at them through the ute window, was looking very relieved too.

Oh well, thought Limpy. At least Christmas hasn't

been a total disaster. At least now we know there's one human in the world with peace and goodwill in his heart.

It's just a shame he's the only one.

By the time Goliath had done his victory dance and finished boasting to some ants about how he'd defeated a ute twice, the firefighter had parked properly and gone into the house.

'Come on,' said Limpy to Goliath. 'We've got a long trip home. Let's grab Uncle Vasco and get started.'

They clambered into the back of the ute.

There, to Limpy's relief, was Uncle Vasco, still safely hidden.

Limpy and Goliath slid their flat sun-baked uncle out from under the coil of rope.

'G'day, Uncle Vasco,' said Goliath. 'Good to see you again.'

Limpy felt the same. He couldn't wait to see Mum and Dad and Charm again too, even though he knew they'd be sad and disappointed when they heard the quest had failed.

'Happy Christmas,' said a cheery voice.

Limpy turned.

A centipede was perched on the coil of rope, pointing at Uncle Vasco with quite a few of its legs.

'I kept an eye on your uncle for you,' said the centipede.

'Thanks,' said Limpy. 'That was very kind.'

'You're worth your weight in dust mites,' said Goliath to the centipede.

'Can't be too careful in this neighbourhood,' said the centipede. 'That brute of a dog next door thinks anything flat and round is a dog biscuit.'

Limpy could believe that.

'The bloke who owns this ute is a worry too,' said the centipede. 'Poor old Stan. He's been doing so much blubbing lately I was worried he'd make your uncle all damp and mouldy.'

Limpy remembered how sad the firefighter had looked when they first saw him in his house.

'Blubbing?' said Limpy. 'Is that the thing humans do with their eyes when they're sad?'

The centipede nodded.

'And when they're embarrassed,' said Goliath. 'Because, for example, a cane toad has just totally defeated their ute.'

'Look over there,' said the centipede. 'Stan's at it again.'

Limpy peeked over the edge of the ute in the direction the centipede was pointing.

Stan had come back out of the house and was standing near the verandah, staring at a shrub with flowers on it. His beard was trembling and his shoulders were shaking and Limpy could see wetness on his cheeks.

So that's blubbing, thought Limpy.

He wondered what could make a tough firefighter so upset.

'Those were his wife's favourite flowers,' said the centipede quietly. 'She died a few days ago.'

Limpy stared at Stan.

He knew what it felt like to have an uncle die, and an aunt, and even a second cousin.

But a wife?

That must be almost as bad as losing a mum or a dad or a sister.

Poor bloke, thought Limpy.

It didn't seem fair. The only human they'd ever met who had Christmas peace and goodwill in his heart, and this awful thing had happened to him.

Limpy watched sadly as Stan put his head into his hands. His beard and shoulders were shaking even more now.

'Yum,' said Goliath's voice.

Limpy looked down.

Goliath was out of the ute, on the ground, happily chomping away.

'This place keeps getting better,' he said. 'The worms here are really big and juicy.'

'Not so loud,' pleaded Limpy. 'There's somebody over there feeling very sad.'

'I'm chewing as quietly as I can,' protested Goliath.

Limpy didn't say any more. Watching Stan was making him feel too sad to argue.

'Be patient, you lot,' Goliath whispered loudly to the worms. 'I'm eating you as fast as I can. The rest of you, while you're waiting, stay away from Mrs Stan's flowers or you're in big trouble.'

Limpy sighed.

'You OK?' said the centipede.

'Poor Stan,' said Limpy. 'I wish I could help him.'

The centipede gave Limpy the sort of look you give one of those wood lice that eats its own brain.

'You're a cane toad,' said the centipede. 'He's a human. You can't help him.'

'Why not?' said Limpy.

'Because he's a mammal,' said the centipede. 'You're an amphibian. The only thing you two have in common is you both do wees and poos. And you both look like you're having an unhappy Christmas.'

Limpy thought about this.

He looked at Stan, head bowed miserably by the shrub, and at Goliath punishing a worm by chewing it twice as many times as normal.

'I still wish I could help Stan,' said Limpy.

The centipede rolled its eyes and quite a few of its legs.

'Dream on,' it said.

'Cheer a human up?' said Goliath, standing in the back of the ute with his hands on his hips. 'Are you crazy? We've tried to be nice to humans, but the mongrels aren't interested.'

Limpy sighed.

It was always risky telling Goliath a new plan. Goliath was brave and adventurous, but sometimes new plans gave him wind.

'Total waste of time,' said Goliath. 'Plus what's in it for us? It's not like he's offering us pizza or a hi-tech military stick-sharpening machine.'

'There's nothing in it for us,' said Limpy. 'A human who was kind to us is feeling sad and lonely on Christmas Day. I just think it would be nice if we could cheer him up a bit.'

'That's the dumbest idea I've ever heard,' said Goliath.

Limpy was glad Stan was back in the house and didn't have to see Goliath carrying on like this.

'Put yourself in Stan's place, Goliath,' said Limpy. 'I know you've got a good heart. I've seen you helping sugar ants back onto their feet after you've finished licking them.'

Goliath gave the centipede an embarrassed glance.

'I only did it once,' he muttered. 'Anyway, sugar ants don't kill you after you've helped them.'

Limpy wasn't sure what Goliath was on about.

'What if Stan kills us after we've cheered him up,' said Goliath. 'Think about it. Think what humans do when they're happy.'

Limpy frowned, puzzled. He could think of a lot of things humans did when they were happy.

'Gardening?' said the centipede. 'Line dancing?'

'Exactly,' said Goliath. 'Humans do hobbies. And what's their favourite hobby? Killing cane toads.'

'And counting legs,' said the centipede. 'They count legs a lot.'

Limpy pointed out to Goliath that Stan didn't seem like the sort of human who killed cane toads as a hobby. Not given all the swerving he'd done to avoid killing the two of them.

Goliath grunted. He didn't seem totally convinced.

Limpy grabbed Goliath's shoulders and looked him in the eyes.

'Remember how sad you felt when Uncle Vasco got squashed?' said Limpy. 'And how much better you felt when me and Charm cheered you up with those dung beetles. The ones that did somersaults.'

Goliath grinned.

'Yeah,' he said. 'They were fun. They tickled for ages after I swallowed them.'

Goliath gave the centipede another embarrassed glance. Limpy kept looking sternly at Goliath.

Slowly Goliath's shoulders drooped.

'All right,' he muttered. 'I suppose we could think about doing a bit of cheering up.'

Limpy gave Goliath a grateful squeeze. He felt like giving his cousin a hug, but he stopped himself. Goliath didn't approve of toads showing their feelings in front of insects.

'How are we gunna cheer him up?' grumbled Goliath.

'By giving him a Christmas present,' said Limpy.

While Goliath thought about this, the centipede stared at Limpy.

'You are crazy,' said the centipede. 'Humans are rich. We're poor. Why would you want to give a human a Christmas present?'

Limpy didn't try to explain. If the centipede didn't understand now, it never would.

Goliath hugged his Christmas sock to his chest.

'All right,' he said to Limpy. 'We'll do it. But that human's not getting my gravel.'

'Don't worry,' said Limpy. 'I've thought of something else we can give him.'

'Oops,' said Limpy.

It wasn't easy, climbing up a kitchen chair with Uncle Vasco on your back, specially when your crook leg kept slipping on the shiny wood.

Goliath was sharing the load, but it was still tricky.

'Don't fall,' grunted Goliath. 'I don't want to have to say goodbye to an uncle and a cousin all at once.'

Limpy gave Goliath a grateful glance. He knew this wasn't easy for Goliath, giving Uncle Vasco away for Christmas, even though there were lots more uncles stacked up at home.

'I won't fall,' said Limpy, trying to ignore the cramp in his leg.

They paused for a breather halfway up the chair.

Limpy peered over at the big brooding shape of Stan, who was sitting at the other side of the kitchen table, shoulders hunched, having his Christmas lunch. He was chewing mournfully, staring at his plate.

'Look at that,' muttered Goliath. 'Chicken nuggets and he's not even enjoying them. How could anyone with their own tummy not enjoy chicken nuggets?'

'Poor bloke,' said Limpy. 'He must miss his wife terribly.'

Limpy made a mental note that when he was old enough to have a wife, he'd try to find one who was tough and strong and wouldn't die even if a truck ran over her.

'Oh well,' said Goliath, peering over at Stan. 'Uncle Vasco'll cheer him up.'

Limpy hoped Goliath was right. Suddenly he was having a fleeting moment of doubt about his choice of gift for Stan.

Was a flat sun-baked uncle the right present for a human who'd just lost a living breathing family member? Would Stan think the present was stupid and pointless?

Limpy peered over at Stan's plate again, and his warts tingled with relief.

Phew.

It was OK.

Stan didn't already have a placemat.

'Come on,' grunted Goliath, heaving Uncle Vasco onto his back. 'Let's get over there before the chicken nuggets are all gone.'

'Wait,' said Limpy. 'If we leave Uncle Vasco here on the chair, out of sight, we can say g'day to Stan first, then give him his gift. Christmas presents are always better if they're a surprise.'

'You're the expert,' said Goliath. 'You know, at Christmas presents. I'm still the expert at stabbing things.'

Finally they made it.

'Oof,' grunted Goliath as they flopped onto the table top. 'I think I popped a wart.'

Limpy's crook leg felt like it was dropping off, but he didn't mind. Some things hurt even more than crook legs. Losing loved ones, for example. He peered up at Stan, who was still staring at the plate and chewing a chicken nugget mournfully.

'Strange,' whispered Limpy. 'You'd think he'd have noticed us by now.'

But he hadn't.

'Hey, weed-face,' yelled Goliath. 'We've got something for you.'

Now he had.

Limpy watched Stan's beard wobble and his mouth fall open as he stared at the two cane toads on his kitchen table.

'Happy Christmas,' said Goliath.

'He doesn't speak our language, remember?' whispered Limpy.

He gave Stan a big friendly Christmas wave, trying not to show how his warts were suddenly prickling with fear.

An awful thought had just hit him. What if humans who were friendly on roads got really cross if you came into their houses without an invitation?

At least Stan wasn't holding a chainsaw, or a tyre lever, or pegs.

But, Limpy saw with a shiver, he was holding a fork.

Limpy waved again. Goliath was waving too, and dribbling mucus onto the table. Limpy hoped Stan understood what a friendly thing that was when a cane toad did it.

Stan was starting to look like he did. His face was still stunned, but his eyes had softened and a tiny smile was tweaking the corners of his mouth.

'It's working,' Limpy said to Goliath. 'Quick, the prezzie.'

They dropped onto their tummies and dangled over the edge of the table and hauled Uncle Vasco up. Once he was on the table top, they propped him against a sauce bottle.

Goliath cleared his throat.

'This is a gift from us to you to ease the pain of your broken heart,' he said to Stan. 'You'd better look after him, or I'll come back and stab you. Happy Christmas.'

Limpy was grateful Stan didn't speak their language.

Stan stared at Uncle Vasco for a long time.

'Maybe we need to show him how to use his present,' Limpy whispered to Goliath. 'He might not know what a placemat is.'

But before Limpy and Goliath could slide Uncle Vasco under Stan's plate, Stan's face crumpled and big drops of water started rolling down his cheeks into his beard.

It took Limpy a few moments to realise what was happening.

On the table, near Stan's plate, was a photo in a frame. Stan's watery eyes were moving from Uncle Vasco to the photo and back again.

Limpy peered more closely at the photo.

And understood.

'Goliath,' he said as his guts went into a swamp-weed-sized knot. 'I think I've made another terrible mistake.'

Limpy sat on the verandah, staring at the ute parked down by the kerb and wishing it had never swerved into his life.

'Don't feel bad,' said Goliath. 'It was a mistake anyone could make. How were we meant to know that Uncle Vasco looks like Stan's wife?'

Limpy sighed.

'It's my fault,' he said. 'I should have remembered that when our lot get squashed, sometimes our faces end up human-shaped.'

'Personally,' said Goliath, 'I don't think Uncle Vasco does look that much like Mrs Stan. OK, the wrinkles are similar, and her eyes were sort of big and close together like Uncle Vasco's, but that's all. She was a human, for swamp's sake. And Uncle Vasco is completely flat.'

'Photos are completely flat,' said Limpy glumly.

He tried desperately to see a good side to it all.

At least Stan had kept Uncle Vasco. But Limpy had a horrible feeling it was just so the poor bloke could gaze lovingly at Uncle Vasco's wrinkles and feel even sadder about his wife.

Limpy sighed again.

He wished he'd never heard of Christmas.

As far as he could see, Christmas was just a time when half the world felt either lonely, or sad, or both.

Limpy was feeling both.

Home felt further away than it ever had. He wondered what Mum and Dad and Charm were doing. Whatever it was, he hoped they weren't doing it on the highway.

Goliath was rummaging in his sock.

'Here,' he said to Limpy. 'Happy Christmas.'

Limpy blinked, surprised.

Goliath was giving him a Christmas present.

Limpy looked up at Goliath's big warty earnest face, and for a moment he felt better. How could anyone stay miserable with a cousin like this?

Then Limpy saw what Goliath had pulled out of his sock. It was plastic, with a windscreen and human numbers on it.

It looked kind of familiar . . .

With a jolt, Limpy remembered.

The mobile phone from the human house.

'Goliath,' he said, shocked. 'You stole it.'

'Swapped it,' said Goliath. 'Those mongrel cats have got our Santa hats.'

Limpy stared at the phone. Why did Christmas have to be so complicated?

'It's a very kind thought, Goliath,' he said. 'But it's not so kind to the humans who own the phone.'

Goliath didn't look like he agreed, or cared, or even understood.

'Humans use their mobiles a lot at Christmas,' said Limpy. 'And not just for ordering ham and turkey pizzas. I've seen it in the ads. Christmas is a big time for humans getting in touch with their loved ones.'

'If you don't want it,' said Goliath grumpily, putting the phone under his arm, 'I'll keep it.'

Limpy realised he and Goliath had a choice. They could go home to their dear swamp, where their loved ones were waiting for them. Or they could try to stop two more humans having a sad and lonely Christmas.

Limpy made the choice.

He knew he would probably have to spend the rest of his life dodging humans and their vicious weapons. And when he was too old to dodge any more, and he had to face his final truck or peg, he knew that one of his last thoughts would be about how he and Goliath had made a sad human smile, just for a moment.

Limpy looked up at the sky.

The sun hadn't set. There was still a bit of Christmas Day left.

He hopped to his feet and gave Goliath a hug.

'Thanks for my present,' he said.

'It's the thought that counts,' said Goliath.

'I know,' said Limpy. 'That's why we're going to keep the thought and take the present back.'

The setting sun threw long shadows down the street.

Two of the shadows clambered out of a stormwater drain. The large shadow hung back. The small shadow gestured urgently to the large shadow to get a move on.

'Do we have to?' grumbled the large shadow.

'Yes,' said the small shadow, and started hopping towards a house with a shed in its backyard.

The large shadow followed, shoulders slumped, a shadow mobile phone tucked under one arm.

As Limpy hopped, he stared at his dark bobbing self on the footpath in front of him.

Experienced shadow experts, he thought, like owls or glow-worms, would probably be thinking I'm an idiot for putting me and Goliath in danger like this. Exposing us to possible violent attack by two humans in imported tracksuits just to return a mobile phone.

Well they'd be wrong.

Limpy tried to remember what Dad always said.

Sometimes you have to do what you know is right, even if you end up being bashed with a coffee-making machine.

Actually, thought Limpy, I'm not sure if Dad has ever said that.

Because Limpy and Goliath weren't Santa's helpers any more, they didn't bother going back into the house through the kitchen fan exhaust pipe.

The cat door was easier.

Limpy forgot it might not be as safe.

'Look out,' hissed Goliath as he led the way in. 'A cat.'

Limpy froze halfway through the door.

Goliath was right. Over in one corner of the kitchen, on the floor, was a familiar fluffy white ball with claws and teeth.

Limpy saw that the cat's eyes were closed. It was lying curled up in a brushed-nylon leopard-skin sleeping pod, its head resting against a cat bowl from which drifted faint sounds of music.

Limpy slipped quietly through the cat door.

'Please,' he whispered to Goliath. 'Don't start a fight.'

'All right,' muttered Goliath. 'That fur-ball's lucky it's Christmas. Let's just dump the phone and clear out.'

'We should put it back where we found it,'

whispered Limpy. 'Up on the kitchen bench. We'll be OK if we're quiet.'

At that moment, a horrible rasping gurgling sound came from the next room.

Limpy froze again.

'What's that noise?' said Goliath. 'Sounds like a cockatoo in a coffee-making machine.'

Limpy had watched a cockatoo spend quite a bit of time in a coffee-making machine at a human camp-site. This sounded very different. More like a second cat getting really furious and indignant after spotting two cane toads who'd barged in without invitations.

The sound got louder.

Goliath took a hop back.

Limpy took a hop forward.

The noise was sounding less like anger and indignation, and more like desperate gasping for breath.

'If I'm not allowed to start a fight,' said Goliath, 'let's get out of here.'

'Wait,' said Limpy. 'I think the other cat might be in trouble.'

Limpy peeped round the dining-room door.

The first thing he saw was a table covered with the leftover bits of a human meal. A big human meal. There were only two plates on the table, but lots of bowls and platters and serving dishes, all with scraps on them. A big turkey skeleton sat in the middle of the table looking like it wasn't having a very good Christmas.

'Wobbling wasp willies,' gasped Goliath over Limpy's shoulder. 'Check out the scraps.'

Limpy was checking out other things. In particular a couch with two humans on it, heads flopped back, mouths open, asleep.

But the gasping-for-breath sound wasn't coming from them.

It was coming, Limpy saw, from the grey cat, who was lying on the floor, fluffy legs sticking out in all directions, mouth open as wide as it would go, gasping and wheezing and gurgling.

'It's got something stuck in its throat,' said Limpy.

He hopped over to the cat and started to reach into the cat's mouth.

Goliath pulled him away.

'Let me,' said Goliath. 'I'm an expert at this.'

Goliath jammed one arm down the cat's throat.

The cat's eyes widened with surprise, then glared angrily at Goliath.

'It's OK,' Limpy whispered to the cat. 'He's an expert.'

Just in case the cat didn't believe him and sank its teeth into Goliath's arm, Limpy put his own hands into the cat's mouth and pushed against the gums to keep its jaws open.

'Can't feel anything,' muttered Goliath, his arm down the cat's throat up to his shoulder. 'I might have to send a dung beetle down to take a look.'

The cat twitched with alarm.

'That's just a figure of speech,' said Limpy to the cat. 'He doesn't mean an actual dung beetle. It'd probably just be a cockroach.'

'Hang on,' said Goliath. 'I've got something.'

He rummaged and grunted and finally slid his arm out of the cat's throat. In his fist was a turkey bone.

The cat gave an indignant meow.

'Do you mind?' it said. 'I was eating that.'

'Don't be embarrassed,' said Goliath. 'I get stuff jammed in my throat all the time. Twigs, lizards, bits of cars. It happens.'

Limpy nodded to the cat to show that it did happen, at least to Goliath.

'What's going on?' said a voice behind them.

Limpy turned.

The white cat was in the doorway, frowning.

'These clowns reckon they saved my life,' said the grey cat. 'As if.'

The white cat narrowed its eyes.

'Were you eating bones again?' it said to the grey cat. 'Did one get stuck again?'

The grey cat looked at the floor.

'One might have got a bit stuck,' it mumbled.

The white cat sighed and shook its head long-sufferingly. After a moment, it squinted at the food scraps on the table, then at Limpy and Goliath.

'Amazing,' said the white cat. 'A pile of food sitting unguarded, and you two aren't up there gutsing yourselves. That's pretty rare for cane toads in my experience, putting a good deed before a good feed.'

Limpy smiled bashfully and glanced at Goliath, who was looking wistfully at the scraps on the table.

'You must let us repay your generosity,' said the white cat. 'What would you like? A musical bowl? A mechanical mouse that's also an MP3 player? Anything, just take it.'

'A big bucket of scraps?' said Goliath.

'I know what I'd like,' said Limpy quietly.

The idea had just hit him like a flying Santa sleigh out of the blue.

'Name it,' said the white cat.

'A human friend of ours is very sad and lonely,' said Limpy. 'If he had a new friend, perhaps he wouldn't feel so alone . . .'

Limpy hesitated.

He couldn't bring himself to say it. He could see how content and well-looked-after the cats were, and it just didn't seem fair to ask one of them to go and live with Stan.

The cats were looking at each other.

'I think I know what you're asking for,' said the white cat to Limpy. 'And the answer is yes.'

Limpy felt a bit stunned.

'That's wonderful,' he croaked.

'Can we have a bucket of scraps as well?' said Goliath.

While the white cat led Limpy towards the other end of the house, Limpy rehearsed a thank-you speech in his head. About how kind it was for one of the cats to leave this comfy home to go and live with a lonely human it hadn't even met.

But before Limpy could say anything, angry voices started hissing behind him.

'Gimme my hat.'

'It's not your hat, it's my blankie.'

'Thieving fluff-ball.'

'Tragically unintelligent wart-head.'

Limpy turned and saw that Goliath and the grey cat were both struggling over something red and white and bobbly and familiar. Goliath had one end of it in his mouth, and the cat was clawing at the other end.

Limpy realised it was one of the Santa hats he and Goliath had left in the shed last night.

'Finders keepers,' protested the grey cat. 'That

means it's mine now, gravel-breath.'

'Mmmf mmp mmg mmf,' retorted Goliath, which Limpy was pretty sure meant, 'Yeah, well I just found it again, fluff-brain.'

'Stop that,' said the white cat loudly.

Goliath and the grey cat stopped wrestling, but neither of them let go of the Santa hat.

The white cat gave the grey cat a stern look.

'Where are your manners?' said the white cat. 'Give our friend his hat.'

The grey cat scowled and let go of the hat.

'Say thank you,' whispered Limpy to Goliath.

Goliath opened his mouth and the hat plopped soggily onto the floor.

'Why should I say thank you?' he grumbled. 'It's mine. Cats don't need hats. Whoever heard of a cat in a hat?'

'It's my blankie,' said the grey cat in a hurt voice.

Limpy didn't like seeing anyone sad on Christmas night.

'There should be another Santa hat around here somewhere,' he said to the grey cat. 'I left mine in the shed last night too. You can have that one for your blankie if you like.'

'Unfortunately,' said the white cat, 'the other hat got thrown out.'

'What?' squeaked Goliath. 'That's an outrage. We risked our warts to get those hats. Who chucked it out?'

'Our owners,' said the white cat. 'They threw

it away after they'd used it to wipe some horrible dribbly stuff off the lawnmower.'

There was a silence.

Limpy decided not to pursue the matter any further, and he could see Goliath was feeling the same.

Anyway, the hats didn't really matter.

What was important was that one of the cats was going to live with Stan.

'This is so kind of you,' Limpy said to the cats. 'Leaving this comfy house to live with a lonely human you haven't even met. Um, which one of you will actually be, you know, going?'

There was a long silence.

Both cats stared at Limpy.

'Leave this comfy house?' said the white cat.

'To live somewhere else?' said the grey cat.

'With a human we haven't even met?' said the white cat.

'Why would we do that?' said the grey cat.

Limpy felt his warts blushing.

'Oh dear,' he said. 'I must have misunderstood. I'm sorry, I thought one of you was offering to go.'

Both cats shook their heads.

'We couldn't possibly leave here,' said the white cat. 'Our owners would be heartbroken.'

'Plus,' said the grey cat, 'they've got two gold-studded flea collars on order from Italy.'

Limpy's warts sagged.

A lovely picture faded from his imagination.

The one of Stan's face beaming. Well, not beaming exactly, but sort of glowing softly behind his beard as the wet stuff dried up.

'We're sorry too,' said the white cat. 'We thought you just wanted to get your human friend another human friend for Christmas.'

'Dangling duck flaps,' exploded Goliath. 'Why would we want to do that?'

Limpy stared at the cats for a moment, taking this in.

His warts started to tingle.

'Actually,' he said, 'that's a very good idea.'

The cats led Limpy and Goliath into a bedroom.

'Wow, look,' said Goliath, putting on the Santa hat and gazing into a mirror. 'The colour of this hat matches some of my wombat teeth marks.'

'Goliath,' whispered Limpy. 'Pay attention. These kind cats are going to help us find Stan a friend.'

The cats jumped up onto a desk with a computer on it.

Limpy knew about computers. He'd seen the ads. He knew they were good for sending messages, and doing other things he couldn't quite remember.

Washing clothes?

'Hey good-looking,' Goliath was saying to his reflection. 'You are hot in that hat.'

Limpy didn't say anything. Sometimes it was better to accept that Goliath lived in a world of his own and leave it at that.

Up on the desk, the cats were tapping the computer keyboard with their claws.

The screen lit up.

Limpy squinted at it.

There was a lot of stuff on it he didn't understand, the stuff humans called print that looked like rows of ants doing yoga. There were also some things Limpy did understand. Photos of humans, including the cats' owners.

'Wow,' said Goliath, hopping up onto the desk and nearly knocking the grey cat off. He gazed at the screen. 'How did you do that?'

Limpy hopped up too, in case Goliath tried to eat the computer.

'We're very intelligent,' said the white cat. 'And we spend a lot of time watching humans.'

'Same here,' said Goliath. 'It's how I learned burping.'

Limpy interrupted before Goliath got on to nose picking.

'Is this how we're going to let the humans know about Stan?' Limpy asked. 'With a computer photo?'

The cats both nodded.

'It's how humans get friends,' said the white cat.

'Really?' said Goliath, looking amazed. 'They don't sniff bottoms?'

'I know it seems weird,' said the white cat. 'But if you're a human and you want friends, you just go on the internet and send out a photo of your face.'

'Brilliant,' said Limpy. He wasn't sure what the internet was, but it sounded amazing.

Then he remembered something.

'We haven't got a photo of Stan,' he said.

The cats looked at each other, and Limpy could tell from their faces that the whole plan had gone a bit hopeless.

'Back soon,' said Goliath, hopping down from the desk.

'World of his own,' said Limpy apologetically to the cats.

The white cat nodded understandingly as if it also had a cousin who tried to stab trucks, which Limpy thought was very kind.

He struggled to remember if he'd seen a photo of Stan anywhere in Stan's house or ute. He was still thinking when Goliath hopped back up onto the desk with the mobile phone.

'Aha,' said the white cat. 'This looks interesting.'

Goliath carefully put the phone down on the desk and punched one of the buttons with his fist. The phone screen lit up.

With a photo of Stan.

Limpy stared.

'I took it to help me remember Uncle Vasco,' said Goliath.

In the photo Stan was sitting at his kitchen table staring wistfully at Uncle Vasco's wrinkles.

'Watching humans didn't just teach me about burping and nose-picking,' said Goliath. 'I also learned about mobile phones. And making duck noises under my arm.'

Limpy was so amazed he could hardly speak.

'You know how to take photos with a phone?' he said to Goliath.

Goliath nodded proudly.

'Watch,' he said.

He put the mobile on its side and posed in front of it with his Santa hat at a jaunty angle.

'Press the big button,' he said.

Limpy pressed it. There was a bright flash and Goliath's photo appeared on the phone screen.

'Stack me,' said Limpy.

'Your cousin's a clever bloke,' said the white cat to Limpy.

'Not just an ugly face,' said the grey cat.

The white cat picked up a computer lead in its mouth, slid the shiny metal end into the back of the phone, and prodded a button until the photos of Stan and Goliath appeared on the computer screen.

'There,' said the white cat after one more click. 'Done.'

Limpy felt a bit dazed.

'That's amazing,' he said. 'Stan's photo has gone out over the internet?'

'And your cousin's,' said the white cat.

'Maybe he'll make a new friend who'll teach him about sharing,' muttered the grey cat.

Limpy put a nervous hand on Goliath's arm.

But it was OK. No fights broke out. Goliath hadn't even heard what the grey cat said. He was too busy gazing at his photo on the computer screen.

'This peace and goodwill caper's not bad,' he said. 'Makes me look really handsome.'

Limpy gave the cats a grateful grin.

'Thanks,' he said. 'And good on you, Goliath. You might just have made a lonely human very happy.'

'He'd better be,' muttered Goliath, 'or I'll stab the mongrel.'

Limpy and Goliath left through the cat door.

'Bye,' Limpy called to the cats. 'Thanks again.'

On the other side of the door, the cats were both waving.

'Thanks for the hat,' called Goliath.

Limpy saw the grey cat mutter something, and the white cat give it a stern glare.

As Limpy and Goliath hopped down the driveway in the moonlight, Limpy heard the mobile phone ringing inside the house. The ring tone was an unusual one. It sounded a bit like the noise a stink beetle makes when you blow into its bottom.

'Goliath,' said Limpy. 'Did you change the ring tone?'

Goliath grinned. 'They just had boring old music,' he said.

Limpy rolled his eyes.

Oh well, at least now the humans in the house would be able to spend Christmas night staying in touch with their loved ones.

Limpy sighed. He wondered how long till he and Goliath would be able do that. Talk to Mum and Dad and Charm.

It could take days to get home.

Weeks even.

And when we finally get there, thought Limpy sadly, I'll have to break the news to the others that humans still aren't our friends.

Limpy pushed the thought away. No point worrying about that yet. First they had to get home.

Limpy and Goliath headed down the street towards the stormwater drain.

They hadn't gone very far when human shouts rang out in the darkness.

Limpy recognised the sort of shouts they were. The delighted ones humans give when they spot a cane toad and are looking forward to a bit of stabbing and squashing.

Which, Limpy thought grimly, humans like to do right through the year, including Christmas night.

'Hop for it,' he said.

While he and Goliath hopped, Limpy looked over his shoulder. He squinted into the haze from the streetlights, trying to see how far away the humans were. Desperately trying to work out if he and Goliath would get to the drain with their inside bits still inside them.

The answer looked like being no.

The yelling humans weren't the cat owners, they were a group of teenagers sprinting out of the front yard of a nearby house.

And they were very close now.

'Goliath,' yelled Limpy. 'Hop faster. Don't wait for me.'

Limpy knew if he hopped any faster himself, his crook leg would make him go round in circles. He wondered if a bit of poison spray from his glands would slow the humans down so Goliath could get away.

'Forget it,' said Goliath, pulling his Santa hat firmly onto his head and staying at Limpy's side. 'I'm not leaving you.'

Limpy's final thought, as he got ready to be squashed and stabbed, and his inside bits got ready to be left dangling from powerlines, was that he was very lucky to have a cousin who was not only quite smart, but also very loving.

Except, to Limpy's surprise, he and Goliath weren't squashed or stabbed.

Instead, Limpy saw something amazing.

The human teenagers were pointing at him and Goliath and shouting and laughing, but not in a cruel way.

In a friendly way.

Limpy stared.

Slowly he realised what was happening.

At last, he thought happily.

Christmas goodwill.

Then a human foot thudded into his warts and he sailed across the street and landed in a hedge.

For a while Limpy was too dazed and sore and upside down to see what was going on. But when he finally sorted out which was his bottom and which was his head, he peered out through the leaves and saw another amazing thing.

The human teenagers had picked Goliath up.

Goliath wasn't spraying them with poison or stabbing them with sticks or doing anything violent.

He looked like he was enjoying himself.

That's odd, thought Limpy. Goliath normally hates being touched by anyone who's not slimy. He must just be feeling relieved because the humans didn't boot him across the street.

One of the teenagers was holding Goliath gently in both hands while the others crowded round, pointing and laughing, still in a friendly way.

Then Limpy noticed something else.

It wasn't so much Goliath the laughing teenagers were pointing at delightedly, it was the Santa hat on his head.

Limpy crept across the dark lawn towards the house where the humans were keeping Goliath prisoner.

As he got closer, he listened anxiously for sounds of pain. When Goliath clamped his teeth onto something, he didn't let go, not even if it was something yucky like a human finger.

But there were no sounds of pain.

Just humans laughing and Goliath burping.

Limpy peered out from behind a bush and saw that the human teenagers were gathered on a deck. Sitting on a table in the middle of them was Goliath, looking pretty happy for a prisoner. The teenagers were patting him on the Santa hat and feeding him bits of food.

'Actually,' said Goliath, 'the turkey's a bit dry. Can we go with some more of the smoked salmon?'

Limpy knew the teenagers couldn't understand what Goliath was saying, but to Limpy's amazement they kept putting food into Goliath's mouth.

I don't get it, thought Limpy. They kick me and feed him. What's going on?

'He looks so cute in that hat,' said one of the teenagers.

'Like a warty little Santa,' said another, patting Goliath's fluffy bobble.

'He's my favourite Facebook friend,' said a third.

Limpy didn't understand the language, but from the grins on all the teenagers' faces, he was pretty sure they were saying something like, 'This is so cool because if we hadn't met this cane toad, we'd have to cart these food scraps all the way out to the garbage bin.'

Limpy frowned.

He still didn't get it.

The garbage bin was right next to the deck.

Limpy sent Goliath an urgent croak, one of the

very low-pitched ones that cane toads can hear but humans can't. Or if they can, they just think their bathroom pipes are blocked.

'Goliath,' the croak said. 'Try to escape. We've got a long trip home.'

Goliath heard it.

Limpy saw him glance over, and then pretend he hadn't heard.

'Any more mango ice-cream?' Goliath said to the teenagers. 'Or gherkins?'

Limpy sighed and sent Goliath another urgent croak.

Finally Goliath ate a very big piece of Christmas cake and threw up.

At last, thought Limpy gratefully.

He waited while the human teenagers groaned in disgust and went indoors, then he hopped out from behind the bush and up onto the deck.

'Come on,' Limpy said to Goliath, who was dozing like he always did when he'd just eaten twice his own body weight.

Goliath didn't argue. Just blinked and scratched his warts and burped a few times and pulled his Santa hat onto his head and followed Limpy out of the backyard.

Limpy tried to remember the way to the stormwater drain.

'That was amazing,' said Goliath as they hopped along the street. 'Those humans went for my rugged warty good looks big time.'

'I've got another theory,' said Limpy.

'My magnetic personality?' said Goliath.

'I think it was the hat,' said Limpy. 'I think that's the mistake we've been making. There is peace and goodwill at Christmas, but to get it you need to wear a Santa hat.'

Goliath took off his Santa hat and frowned at it.

'Nah,' he said. 'I reckon it was my good looks.'

Limpy didn't argue.

He was too busy going rigid with alarm.

Two humans, a man and a woman, were walking arm in arm towards them along the street.

'Quick,' said Limpy, hopping into the gutter and peering frantically around for the stormwater drain.

Goliath lifted him back onto the footpath.

'What are you doing?' said Limpy.

'Checking out your theory,' said Goliath.

He put the Santa hat onto Limpy's head, then waved and yelled at the human couple, who were quite close now.

'Hey, smoothies,' he shouted. 'Who do you like better, me or the skinny kid in the hat?'

'Goliath,' pleaded Limpy. 'This isn't a good idea.'

But Goliath wasn't listening. Specially not after the man's boot thudded into his warts and sent him howling across the street into a hedge.

'That doesn't prove anything,' grunted Goliath as Limpy brushed twigs and bird poo off him.

'I think it does,' said Limpy.

'It's my looks and personality they go for,' said

Goliath, studying his reflection in the window of a corner shop.

'I think it's the hat,' said Limpy. 'I think humans only feel Christmas peace and goodwill when they see a Santa hat.'

Goliath shook his head.

'That's dopey,' he said. 'And I'm gunna prove it to you. Stay here.'

He steered Limpy into the shadow of the shop doorway, then hopped back out onto the footpath. The light from a street lamp made the warts on his bare head twinkle.

Limpy saw that another human, a man wearing white shorts and carrying a tennis racquet, was strolling along the street towards Goliath.

'Goliath,' begged Limpy. 'Take the hat, please.'

Goliath ignored him.

Limpy couldn't look. He turned away. But he could still hear.

'G'day, mate,' he heard Goliath say. 'Get any good pizzas for Christmas?'

Then a swish.

Then a howl.

'I don't believe it,' said Goliath, crawling back into the shop doorway. 'He whacked me. Just cause I wasn't wearing the dumb hat.'

Goliath winced as he tried to straighten a couple of bent warts on his head.

'Me,' said Goliath, 'with my dazzling personality.'

'Are you convinced now?' said Limpy as he dusted Goliath down again.

'No,' grunted Goliath. 'I reckon that human was a psycho. I'm gunna test this dumb theory one more time.'

Before Limpy could stop him, Goliath grabbed the Santa hat and put it on. Then he hopped towards another group of humans coming along the street. Two grown-ups and several kids, laughing and chatting with armfuls of presents.

'Be careful, Goliath,' whispered Limpy anxiously as he hopped back into the shop doorway.

He heard Goliath yelling at the humans.

'You're all idiots,' shouted Goliath, ' and you can't hop and your yucky smooth skin makes you look like prawns.'

Limpy heard the humans making happy friendly noises.

He heard Goliath yell more insults.

But only for a while.

Then Limpy heard loud chewing sounds.

As soon as the human chatter had faded into the distance, Limpy hopped anxiously out of the doorway.

Goliath, still wearing the Santa hat, was standing in the middle of the footpath, chewing.

And frowning.

'Amazing,' he said. 'I did my best insults to those mongrels and they still let me choose a present.'

He swallowed and burped.

'I chose a yummy toilet deodorant block,' he said.

'And . . . ?' said Limpy, waiting for Goliath to admit it was the hat that had done it.

'Those mongrels must be psycho too,' said Goliath.

It took a long time to find a stormwater drain.

This was mostly because Limpy and Goliath only had the one Santa hat between them. Which meant only one of them could wear it. Which meant that all the humans they met were only nice to one of them.

Which finally convinced Goliath.

'I was right,' he said. 'It is the hat.'

Goliath gobbled a fistful of lollies and posed so some human kids in the back of a car could take his photo in the Santa hat.

Limpy groaned as he crawled out of the pothole he'd dived into when the car tried to run him over.

Why did Goliath take so long to grasp an idea?

It's not really his fault, thought Limpy. He just gets a bit distracted by lollies and Christmas cake and ice-cream and deodorant blocks and gherkins.

The car drove off.

'Come on,' said Limpy, pointing across the street. 'Here's a stormwater drain at last.'

'I've had an idea,' said Goliath. 'Let's make Stan a Christmas card. With a picture that shows him he won't be lonely if he gets himself a Santa hat.'

'Good idea,' said Limpy.

Then he told Goliath the idea he'd had.

'Wouldn't it be wonderful,' said Limpy, 'if we all had Santa hats.'

'What,' said Goliath, 'me and you and Stan?'

'All of us,' said Limpy. 'Mum and Dad and Charm and everyone.'

He watched as Goliath's eyes went wide at the thought.

'I reckon,' said Limpy, 'if we did, humans would be our friends for ever.'

'I still don't understand where we're gunna get heaps and heaps of Santa hats,' said Goliath as he and Limpy hopped across Stan's front yard in the moonlight.

Limpy didn't reply.

He wasn't sure himself.

All he knew was that if he could get a Santa hat onto the head of every cane toad in the swamp, flat rellies would be a thing of the past.

Goliath stopped hopping and took his Santa hat off.

'We could all share this one,' he said. 'Boys one day, girls the next. Kids on even days, grown-ups on odd days. If your birthday's in the second half of the month you divide the number of warts on your left buttock into the number of swamp slugs you can fit into your mouth and subtract . . .'

Goliath's calculations trailed off.

Limpy knew why. One hat among them all

would never work. Plus there was something else he wanted to do with Goliath's Santa hat.

'I want to leave this one with Stan,' said Limpy. 'So he knows what's he's looking for when he goes to get one that'll fit him.'

Goliath didn't reply. He just stared past Limpy, eyes big and unblinking.

For a moment Limpy thought Goliath had hurt his brain trying to do maths. Then he became aware of a scary noise. A growling slobbering noise that didn't sound like happy Christmas in anyone's language.

Limpy turned.

And almost fainted.

Towering over him was the huge dog from next door, angry red eyes glaring, massive teeth glinting wet in the moonlight.

'H-hello,' stammered Limpy. 'Er, how did you get over the fence?'

'My owner got a trampoline for Christmas,' rumbled the dog.

Limpy gulped.

He could feel Goliath trembling next to him.

'Right,' said Limpy. 'Um, about last time, when you might have heard my cousin call you dog-breath and a mongrel and say something about you being history. He's very sorry. We both are.'

The dog scowled, which amazed Limpy.

He'd thought the dog was scowling before.

'That's not what I want to talk to you about,' growled the dog.

'Oh, r-right,' stammered Limpy. 'Is there something else we should be saying sorry about?'

'Yes,' rumbled the dog. 'Him.'

Limpy peered, trying to see what the dog was pointing at.

It was a puppy, not much bigger than Goliath, standing in the big dog's shadow. The puppy had a ribbon tied round its neck.

'Hello,' said the puppy.

'Hello,' said Limpy, desperately wondering what he should be saying sorry for. The ribbon? All the gravel Goliath had eaten? The fire they'd caused at the shopping mall? Perhaps the puppy had wanted to meet Santa and couldn't because of the fire.

It didn't seem likely.

'This little fella's my nephew,' growled the dog. 'Today was going to be his big day. A Christmas present for a loving family in the next street. And it was all fine until you wart-heads came along.'

'I don't understand,' said Limpy.

The dog suddenly lunged at Goliath, huge jaws open.

For a horrible moment, Limpy thought it was the end for Goliath. So did Goliath, judging by the puddle that suddenly appeared at his feet.

But the dog just grabbed the Santa hat, ripped it apart and flung it to the ground.

'We don't like Christmas either,' squeaked Goliath. 'We hate it.'

'That's not what I've heard,' rumbled the dog.

'And because you two clowns have been parading around the district like warty little Santas, no kid in this town wants a puppy for Christmas any more. They all want cane toads in Santa hats.'

Limpy's mind was a whirl.

This was fantastic news.

Then he saw that the dog was looking even angrier.

'Which is why this evening,' rasped the dog, 'my little nephew here was dumped.'

'Oh,' said Limpy, realising the news wasn't quite so good after all. 'Oh dear. We are sorry. Very, very sorry.'

'Sorry's not enough,' growled the dog.

'Extremely humungously sorry?' squeaked Goliath.

'I don't want grovelling,' rumbled the dog. 'I want action. Find this little fella a loving human home. Tonight.'

Limpy gulped again. Perhaps if they put the Santa hat on the puppy . . . ?

No good. The Santa hat was in shreds.

'J-just for our information,' stammered Limpy, 'if we can't find your nephew a loving human home, you know, tonight . . .'

'I'll kill you,' said the dog.

Limpy and Goliath peered in through Stan's kitchen window.

'Yes,' whispered Limpy. 'I think it's working.'

Stan was sitting in his usual spot at the kitchen table. But he wasn't staring tearfully at the photo of his wife. He wasn't even gazing wistfully at Uncle Vasco's wrinkles.

He was feeding chicken nuggets to the puppy, who was sitting on his knee. The puppy was wagging its tail. Stan was chuckling.

'That is a wonderful sight,' said Limpy.

'I know,' said Goliath. 'Aren't chicken nuggets beautiful?'

'Bouncing bushflies,' said an alarmed voice near Limpy's head. 'Is that a dog?'

Limpy saw a familiar-looking spider lowering itself from a verandah beam. The spider was staring into the kitchen, horrified.

'It's a puppy,' said Goliath proudly. 'We gave it to Stan for Christmas.'

'Well,' said Limpy, trying to be truthful, 'not so much gave it, as helped it in through the window.'

'You idiots,' said the spider. 'You realise what you've done, don't you?'

'Stan was lonely,' said Limpy. 'And the puppy was homeless.'

'Great,' said the spider. 'So now I've got to share my home with a dog, one of the most vicious spider-eating species on the planet.' The spider paused and frowned. 'Or is that possums?'

'Don't ask me,' said Goliath. 'Do I look like an information website?'

The spider looked more closely at Goliath, and

Limpy saw its eyes widen as it remembered it had met Goliath before, and that Goliath was a spider-eating species too.

'It's OK,' said Limpy to the spider. 'Relax. You're safe with us. Happy Christmas.'

'Actually,' said the spider, backing away from Goliath, 'it's after midnight, so to be completely accurate it's not Christmas any more, it's Boxing Day.'

Limpy stared at the spider.

Boxing Day?

Limpy tried to remember why Boxing Day sounded familiar.

Of course. The Christmas beetle's girlfriend had told him about it once. Boxing Day was a really important part of Christmas, mostly because of one particular thing.

Limpy's warts tingled with excitement as he remembered what that thing was. And why Boxing Day was the very best day of the year for getting a swamp-load of Santa hats.

The Boxing Day sales.

The next morning, after a sleep in the back of the ute, Limpy and Goliath were at the kitchen window again, peeping in.

'Yes,' said Limpy. 'Perfect.'

'Is that the Boxing Day sales?' said Goliath, craning his neck for a better look.

'No,' said Limpy. 'Well, kind of.'

Stan was sitting at the kitchen table, his beard white and fluffy in the morning sunlight. He was cuddling the puppy and studying a newspaper.

'He's reading ads for the sales,' said Limpy.

'Oh, right, yes, I knew that,' said Goliath.

There was a pause while Limpy watched Stan, and Goliath frowned.

'These Boxing Day sales,' said Goliath. 'Can you eat them?'

Limpy sighed. Sometimes Goliath's thirst for knowledge was exhausting.

Keeping his voice low, Limpy explained to

Goliath how on the day after Christmas all the big stores cut their prices. And all the humans rushed to buy things cheaply. Specially things they wanted for Christmas but didn't get.

'Like pizza?' said Goliath.

'And other things,' said Limpy.

He also explained that sometimes, even when you did get what you wanted for Christmas, you had to buy extra things to go with it.

'Like extra cheese and pepperoni?' said Goliath.

Limpy decided it was quicker to agree.

'Yes,' he said. 'And if what you got was a puppy, you need to buy extra things like a kennel and a lead and a puppy bed and some puppy food.'

Goliath's face lit up with understanding.

'And if what you got for Christmas was an automatic lint-remover,' he said, 'you need to buy some lint.'

Limpy didn't have time to answer. What he had hoped would happen was now happening. Stan was on his feet, reaching across the table for his car keys.

'Brilliant,' said Limpy. 'Stan's going to the sales. Quick, back to the ute.'

'Why is it brilliant?' said Goliath as they hurried across the front yard.

'Because the sales are at the shopping mall,' said Limpy. 'And that's where we can get Santa hats.'

As the ute chugged down the street, Limpy and Goliath stayed hidden in the back as usual.

'I know why we're not riding up front,' said Goliath. 'It's because Stan might decide he'd rather have us as pets and dump the puppy.'

Limpy smiled sadly and shook his head.

'Humans want pets with fur,' he said, 'not warts.'

'Crazy,' said Goliath. 'Anyway, we can't be pets. We're wild creatures of the swamp who are noble and free. Plus we need a constant supply of fresh mud to cool our bottoms when we've been eating spicy gumnuts.'

Limpy nodded. Goliath was right.

And the swamp was exactly the reason Limpy had decided to stay hidden. He needed time to think.

There was one part of the plan he hadn't worked out yet. The most important part. How he and Goliath were going to get back home.

'I am so grateful to you blokes,' said a friendly voice.

Limpy looked up. It was the centipede.

'That was genius,' said the centipede. 'Giving Stan that puppy for Christmas. That brute of a dog next door, I've never seen him so happy. Well, not exactly happy, but he hasn't killed anything for hours.'

'Just a little idea we had,' said Goliath. 'Glad to help.'

'Stan loves that puppy,' said the centipede. 'Won't let it out of his sight. I reckon he'll take it with him when he goes to visit his wife this afternoon.'

'His wife?' said Limpy, confused. 'But she's dead.'

'She's buried in the next town,' said the centipede. 'He goes every day.'

Limpy stared at the centipede. Goliath did too.

'Let me get this straight,' Goliath said to the centipede. 'Humans don't stack dead rellies in their bedrooms, they bury them?' He thought about this. 'Fair enough, I do the same sometimes with my dead warts.'

Limpy barely heard what Goliath was saying. His mind was racing back to when they first met Stan on the highway. Limpy had often wondered where Stan was driving back from that day.

'This next town,' Limpy asked the centipede. 'Is it along the highway to the west?'

'Yes,' said the centipede. 'Do you know it?'

'I don't know the town,' said Limpy, his warts throbbing with excitement. 'But I know the highway. It's where our swamp is.'

'Anyway,' the centipede gushed on, 'we in the front yard and ute community are very grateful to you both, so if there's anything we can do to repay you, just say it.'

Limpy saw Goliath open his mouth.

He slapped his hand over it before Goliath could say anything about pizza.

'Actually,' said Limpy, 'there is something . . .'

The car park was even more crowded than on Christmas Eve. Stan had to park the ute round the back of the shopping mall.

'Disgraceful,' muttered Goliath. 'We're regulars here. We shouldn't have to park out the back with the garbage skips.'

But Limpy didn't mind.

As he waited for Stan and the puppy to head off into the mall, and for the centipede to head off to do the things he'd asked it to do, he rubbed his hands together happily.

This was exactly where he wanted to be.

The metal garbage skip was hot in the sun, and by the time Limpy had climbed up the side his warts were toasted and throbbing.

But not as throbbing as his insides when he finally perched on the rim and looked down into the skip.

Yes.

This was exactly what he'd hoped would be here.

A huge pile of broken plastic Christmas tree branches and tangled fairy lights and charred socks and smashed whatsits and unwell-looking Santa dolls and, mixed up with it all, loads and loads of Santa hats.

Anxiously, Limpy peered at the Santa hats more closely.

Some were a bit burned round the edges, or torn, or streaked with melted plastic, but lots of them were fine.

'Good on you, Limpy,' gasped Goliath as he

peered into the skip. 'You've done it. You've found me a lifetime supply of Santa hats.'

'Not just you, Goliath,' said Limpy happily. 'Everyone.'

Dragging the Santa hats out of the skip took ages.

Carrying them in bundles over to the ute took a while too, even though Limpy was amazed how many Goliath could fit into his mouth at once.

Stacking them in the back of the ute wasn't a quick job either.

But Limpy discovered that luckily humans don't look around much in car parks when they're hurrying towards shopping malls anxious not to miss bargains. And when a mall is packed, it takes a bloke with a puppy ages to buy a kennel and a lead and a puppy bed and puppy food. Specially when he's meeting lots of new Facebook friends.

'Finished,' panted Limpy as he and Goliath stacked the last hats in the back of the ute.

'I don't want to ruin your Boxing Day,' said Goliath, frowning. 'But I've just thought of something. How are we gunna get Stan to stop at the swamp and drop us off when we don't speak his language?'

'Don't worry,' said Limpy. 'It'll be fine.'

He glanced over to the other end of the ute, where the centipede and its friends had almost finished getting things ready.

By the time they had, Stan was approaching.

Limpy could tell it was Stan. At first glance it looked like a huge pile of parcels on legs, but Limpy could see the puppy trotting alongside on a new lead.

'OK,' said Limpy to Goliath. 'Help me get Stan's attention.'

When the pile of parcels had almost reached the ute, Limpy and Goliath started yelling and waving.

'G'day Stan,' shouted Limpy. 'We're down here. There's something we want to show you.'

'Hey, fuzzy face,' yelled Goliath. 'It's us. Santa's ex-helpers.'

It was the puppy who saw them first. After it barked happily and wagged its tail for a while, Stan's face appeared over the parcels, staring at Limpy and Goliath in amazement.

Limpy didn't waste any time.

He pointed to the other end of the ute, to where the centipede was waiting. Stan shifted his gaze, and Limpy gave the centipede the signal to start.

The centipede had done a really good job.

Painted onto the metal floor of the ute was a smear of black engine grease that looked exactly like a miniature section of the highway. Squatting side-by-side on the little highway were two fat beetles. Limpy could see them puffing their chests out to look more like cane toads.

Best of all was the centipede.

Stuck onto its back was an old piece of bubble-gum in the shape of a ute. At Limpy's signal, the centipede ute started scampering along the little highway towards the two cane-toad beetles.

'I don't get it,' said Goliath. 'What's going on?'

'You'll see,' whispered Limpy. 'It's to jog Stan's memory so he'll know where to drop us off on his way to see his wife this afternoon.'

Limpy held his breath. For a while it looked as though the centipede ute was going to drive straight over the cane-toad beetles and squash them flat. But at the last moment, the ute swerved and missed them.

Brilliant, thought Limpy. If that doesn't remind Stan where he swerved off the road near our place, I'm a warty placemat.

Limpy wanted to applaud.

But he didn't. Instead he looked hopefully up at Stan.

And saw, to his disappointment and dismay, that Goliath wasn't the only one who didn't have a clue what was going on.

Stan didn't either.

That afternoon Stan drove to the next town to visit his wife's grave.

In the back of the ute, Limpy was rolling around as usual. This time so was Goliath.

Limpy managed to grab hold of the spare tyre and stop rolling long enough to peer out at the highway.

It was a long way down. Plus the ute was going so fast, the bitumen was just a blur.

'Are you sure you're OK about this?' he said to Goliath.

'What?' said Goliath, rolling past. 'Risking our lives to get home?'

Limpy nodded.

'You didn't say anything about it being so uncomfortable,' grumbled Goliath, rolling back. 'I'm melting in these hats.'

'Sorry,' said Limpy.

He was feeling pretty overheated too. But you had to expect that when you were wearing so many

Santa hats. Specially when they were all wrapped round you in a big ball.

'I think this is it,' yelled the centipede, who was clinging to the roof of the driver's cab, peering at the highway ahead.

Limpy squinted ahead himself.

Yes.

The centipede was right.

Coming up was the railway crossing near the swamp.

'This is it,' Limpy said to Goliath, who was still rolling around. 'Get ready to jump.'

Limpy dragged himself up onto the spare tyre.

Eventually Goliath joined him.

'It's going to be OK,' said Limpy, hoping that the wind battering his face wasn't whipping his croaks away before Goliath could hear them. 'Try to forget that jumping from a ute at this speed would normally result in instant death. We'll be fine. We're wrapped up in so many layers of Santa hats, we won't even feel it. We'll just bounce a few times and roll a bit.'

'So there's no need to be scared?' said Goliath.

'Absolutely not,' said Limpy.

They jumped.

'Arghhh,' yelled Limpy, terrified.

Goliath was yelling too.

For a few moments they were flying, spinning in mid-air, buffeted by the wind, giddy and out of control.

Limpy hoped he wouldn't be sick on the Santa hats.

Then he hit the road.

He'd been wrong. He did feel it.

A lot.

He felt it more with each bounce.

After a lot of bounces, the rolling started. There was a lot of rolling too, but finally, when it stopped, Limpy opened his eyes.

He was lying in the long grass next to the highway, quite close to the swamp. The Santa hats were still attached to him. So were his arms and legs, as far as he could tell.

He heard a loud groan from nearby.

'I'm never doing that again,' croaked a grumpy voice.

Limpy rolled over and peered around. And saw with relief that Goliath was in one piece too. He was wedged in a thorn bush, and muttering rude words, but his outer layer of Santa hats was still intact.

Then another voice rang out through the swamp weed.

'Limpy. Goliath.'

Limpy rolled over and grinned.

It was Charm, hopping towards them, her dear little face glowing with delight. Behind her, just as delighted, were Mum and Dad.

'Look, Mum and Dad,' said Charm. 'It's Limpy and Goliath. Santa brought them home in his ute.'

'Limpy,' said Mum, hugging as much of him as

she could get her arms round. 'Thank swamp you're safe. Gee, you've put on a bit of weight.'

Limpy didn't try to explain about the Santa hats.

Not for a while.

For now he just wanted to lie here and enjoy Charm's cuddles, and watch Mum and Dad pulling Goliath out of the thorn bush and pulling thorns out of Goliath.

He wanted to let it all sink in.

They were home.

Limpy stood in the moonlight in the middle of the highway with Goliath and Charm and Mum and Dad, holding his breath.

This was the moment of truth.

'Limpy,' said Dad quietly. 'Whether or not this works, I just want you to know I'm proud of you for going on this quest, and I'm proud of you for trying to bring human friendship to cane toads for countless generations to come. And the same for you, Goliath.'

'So am I,' said Mum.

'And me,' said Charm.

Limpy gave them all a grateful look.

'Limpy,' said Charm. 'The car's still ages away. Breathe.'

Limpy took a breath.

And held it again.

The car wasn't that far away. He could see its headlights getting closer and closer.

For the millionth time, Limpy peered around at all the cane toads on the highway to make sure every single one of them had a Santa hat on his or her head.

They did.

Limpy tried to feel relaxed.

It was hard. Some of the toads weren't even looking at the car. They were busy looking at the flying insects they were having for dinner. The dinners were complaining as usual.

'Christmas spirit?' the flying insects were saying, peering out of various mouths at various Santa hats. 'Don't make us laugh.'

The headlights were very close now.

Please work, Limpy pleaded silently.

'It'd better work,' muttered Goliath, adjusting his Santa hat and gripping his stick, 'or I'm gunna start stabbing.'

Suddenly the cane toads on the highway were completely lit up in the glare from the headlights. Limpy knew the driver could see them, and their Santa hats.

He waited for the driver to feel a surge of Christmas peace and goodwill.

To swerve.

To not drive over any cane toads.

It didn't happen.

The driver swerved, but directly towards a group of rellies.

'Look out,' screamed Limpy.

Cane toads scattered in all directions. Limpy grabbed Mum and Dad and dragged them away from the car. He saw Goliath with Charm on his shoulders, pushing toads to safety with one hand and hurling his stick at the car with the other.

The car hissed past and roared away into the night.

'Where's your Christmas spirit, you bully,' yelled Charm at the disappearing rear lights.

'Mongrel,' yelled Goliath.

Limpy looked fearfully at the surface of the highway, wondering how many patches of squashed rellie he'd see.

It was a miracle.

There weren't any.

But Limpy knew it wasn't because of the Santa hats. It was just luck.

He put his head in his hands.

The Santa hats hadn't worked.

Why?

At dawn, after Limpy wearily finished his lookout shift on the ant hill, he went to see the Christmas beetle, hoping for an explanation.

The Christmas beetle had one.

'Christmas is over, dopey.'

Limpy didn't understand.

'But it's still the Christmas holiday period,' he said.

He waited while the Christmas beetle did some

exasperated head-shaking and eye-rolling.

'What did you expect?' said the Christmas beetle. 'Christmas cheer till August? Forget it. Humans are busy. They've got Easter and Mothers Day and Halloween to think about. Those hats'll protect you for one day a year, two tops.'

Later, as Limpy flopped onto his bed, Charm came in with another explanation.

She was dragging a newspaper that had been left at a picnic site that day.

Limpy stared at the page she was pointing to.

He couldn't understand the headline, or the columns of ant yoga, but from the photo he could tell it was a report about the shopping mall fire. Limpy knew what human newspapers were like, so he guessed the report had an angry theory about who or what had started the fire.

The photo showed the wrecked and burning Christmas tree.

The angry and outraged shoppers.

And in the middle of it all, staring out of the photo, bits of a Christmas angel on his head, was Goliath.

'Oh no,' moaned Limpy. 'They know we were involved.'

Suddenly it all seemed hopeless. All the risks, all the danger, all the effort he and Goliath had put into their quest, and now humans hated cane toads even more than before.

Accidently burn down one Christmas tree,

thought Limpy bitterly, and they never forgive you.

'You tried,' whispered Charm, pressing her little face against his tummy.

'We did,' said Limpy miserably. 'But it was a complete waste of time.'

The next afternoon, while Limpy was sitting by the swamp gazing sadly into the water, Charm appeared, her little warts glowing with excitement.

'Limpy,' she said. 'Santa's come to see you.'

Limpy stared at her.

Then he jumped up and hopped after her towards the highway.

Goliath was already there, in the long grass next to the road, with something that made Limpy's warts perk up with pleasure.

Stan's ute, and Stan, and the puppy.

'G'day,' said a familiar voice.

It was the centipede, perched on the edge of the ute with its two beetle friends.

'We did another performance of the highway swerving demonstration this morning,' said the centipede. 'This time Stan got it.'

Stan was grinning, happier than Limpy had ever seen him.

Limpy gave the centipede a grateful hug, even though he knew Goliath didn't like cane toads showing their feelings in front of insects. Then he saw Goliath was giving the two beetles a hug.

Stan handed round some chicken nuggets.

'Thanks Uncle Limpy and Uncle Goliath,' said the puppy, licking them both on the warts. 'You were right, I really like Uncle Fuzzy Face.'

Limpy gave the puppy a stern look.

'That's just a name Uncle Goliath made up,' said Limpy. 'His real name is Uncle Stan.'

'I like that better,' said the puppy. 'Thanks.'

After a while, Limpy saw Stan looking at his watch, which Limpy guessed was a thing humans did when they were worried about being late for visiting times at cemeteries.

Limpy and Goliath said goodbye to the centipede and the beetles and the puppy.

Saying goodbye to Stan was harder.

Limpy could see that Stan had lots of things he wanted to say. Limpy had a few too, mostly thanking Stan for devoting his life to fighting bushfires, and giving him some more sympathy about his wife, and inviting Stan to meet Limpy's wife once Limpy had met her himself.

But of course none of those things could be said.

It didn't matter.

When Stan crouched and gently shook Limpy and Goliath by the hand, Limpy could tell from Stan's warm smile that language wasn't really needed.

And when Stan lifted Uncle Vasco from the cabin of the ute and laid him gently on the grass in front of Limpy and Goliath, Limpy knew what Stan's eyes were saying.

Thank you.

Stan got back into the ute and started it up.

Limpy waved while Stan reversed onto the highway. Stan and the puppy and the insects waved back.

As the ute drove off, Limpy had a lot of sad goodbye feelings, but he also had a very happy thought.

The mission hadn't been a complete waste of time after all.

Limpy lay in a lovely cool mud hole and gazed up at the beautiful night sky.

A shooting star grazed the twinkling heavens.

Or perhaps it wasn't a shooting star.

'I wonder if that's Santa?' said Limpy. 'On his way home.'

Goliath grunted. 'I don't believe in Santa any more,' he muttered. 'Or his ute.'

'I do,' said Charm. 'Look, if you squint a bit, you can see the reindeer.'

The three of them lay in comfortable silence for a while.

Then Limpy gave a big sigh.

'Oh Limpy,' said Charm. 'You're not still feeling bad about the quest, are you? You shouldn't. You did your best.'

'We did better than our best,' said Goliath.

'I'm not feeling bad,' said Limpy. 'I'm sighing because I'm feeling so happy.'

And he was.

As he gazed up at the stars, Limpy thought about what an interesting Christmas it had been, full of surprises. A Santa who turned out to be a firefighter. An automatic lint-remover that turned out to be a lawnmower. A killer dog who turned out to be a big help.

And even though the quest wasn't a total success, thought Limpy, there'll probably be others, and one of them might be.

That thought made him happy.

So did something else.

Charm gave Limpy a muddy hug. Goliath gave him a muddy slug cutlet. Limpy gazed across the swamp to where Mum and Dad were relaxing in their own mud hole.

Tonight his family was safe and he was home with them.

What better Christmas present could you ask for than that?

ALSO BY MORRIS GLEITZMAN

TOAD RAGE

The epic story of one slightly squashed cane toad's quest for the truth.

TOAD HEAVEN

The stirring saga of one slightly squashed cane toad's dreams of a safe place and what happens when he wakes up.

TOAD AWAY

The heroic tale of one slightly squashed cane toad's travels across oceans, continents and some really busy roads.

ALSO BY MORRIS GLEITZMAN

GIVE PEAS A CHANCE

Fifteen funny tales, featuring a host of Morris's beloved characters and some new ones. While Ginger and her dog Anthony organise the ultimate party, Wilton the tummy worm meets Aristotle the nose germ in an unexpected location and Ben tries to save the world by not eating his vegetables.

DOUBTING THOMAS

The truth is . . . Thomas has an embarrassing secret. Is it a rare and special gift or the worst thing that could happen to a boy? A story about best friends, surprising adventures and itchy nipples.

AVAILABLE FROM PUFFIN

ALSO BY MORRIS GLEITZMAN

BOY OVERBOARD

Jamal and Bibi have a dream. To lead Australia to soccer glory in the next World Cup.

But first they must face landmines, pirates, storms and assassins. Can Jamal and his family survive their incredible journey and get to Australia?

GIRL UNDERGROUND

Bridget wants a quiet life. Including, if possible, keeping her parents out of prison. Then a boy called Menzies makes her an offer she can't refuse, and they set off on a job of their own. It's a desperate, daring plan – to rescue two kids, Jamal and Bibi, from a desert detention centre. Can Bridget and Menzies pull off their very first jail break, or will they end up behind bars too?

ALSO BY MORRIS GLEITZMAN

TEACHER'S PET

Ginger is named after a cat. Some people reckon she's more like the fierce stray dog she takes to Pet's Day. Ginger tries to be good, but it's not easy when your mum puts cat food in your breakfast bowl. It gets even harder when the school principal is trying to kill your best friend.

ADULTS ONLY

Jake's an only kid. He's the only kid in his family. He's the only kid on his island. Or that's what he thinks . . . A funny and surprising story about new and old friends.

WATER WINGS

Where do you get a top gran at short notice? It's not easy, but Pearl's got Winston to help her, and you can do anything when your best friend is the world's brainiest guinea pig. Then Pearl meets Gran and the surprises begin.

AVAILABLE FROM PUFFIN

ALSO BY MORRIS GLEITZMAN

WICKED!

(with Paul Jennings)

Slurping slobberers want to suck their bones out. Strange steel sheep want to smash them to pieces. Giant frogs want to crunch them up. Their parents can't help them. Dawn and Rory are on their own.

DEADLY!

(with Paul Jennings)

Join Amy and Sprocket as they desperately search for their families – a quest that will take them to the weirdest nudist colony in the world. Uncovering deadly secret after deadly secret, they are lured deeper into an exciting mystery.

ALSO BY MORRIS GLEITZMAN

WORM STORY

The hilarious tale of two tiny parasites and their very big adventure.

ARISTOTLE'S NOSTRIL

Aristotle just wants to be happy. Is that too much for a germ to ask?

SECOND CHILDHOOD

It looks like Mark's heading for oblivion. Until he and his friends discover they've lived before. Not only that – they were Famous and Important People!

THE OTHER FACTS OF LIFE

Ben's dad has told him the facts of life. But it's the other facts that are worrying Ben and he decides to find out his own answers. He's deadly serious – and the results are very, very funny.

AVAILABLE FROM PUFFIN

ALSO BY MORRIS GLEITZMAN

GIFT OF THE GAB

It starts off as a normal week for Rowena. A car full of stewed apples. A police cell. A desperate struggle to keep Dad off national TV. Then her world turns upside-down. And suddenly Ro is battling French policemen, high explosives and very unusual sausages to discover painful and joyous secrets that change her life forever. The hilarious heart-stopping climax to *Blabber Mouth* and *Sticky Beak.*

BUMFACE

His mum calls him Mr Dependable, but Angus can barely cope. Another baby would be a disaster. So Angus comes up with a bold and brave plan to stop her getting pregnant. That's when he meets Rindi. And Angus thought *he* had problems . . .

AVAILABLE FROM PUFFIN

ALSO BY MORRIS GLEITZMAN

BLABBERMOUTH

Rowena wants to be friends but the other kids don't. Is it because she's stuffed a frog into Darryn Peck's mouth? Or is it because of her dad?

STICKY BEAK

The last thing Rowena wants in her life right now is a cockatoo with a crook temper. She's got enough problems of her own. But a crazy cockatoo, Ro discovers, can be just the friend she needs. The funny and poignant sequel to *Blabbermouth*.

TWO WEEKS WITH THE QUEEN

A story of extraordinary power and poignancy. A heart-warming novel for young and old alike that has become an international best-seller, justly famed for its humour and emotion.

AVAILABLE FROM PAN MACMILLAN

ALSO BY MORRIS GLEITZMAN

MISERY GUTS

What does a kid do when his mum and dad are misery guts? Move them to a tropical paradise, decides Keith. That'll cheer them up. It's a brilliant plan – if he can pull it off.

WORRY WARTS

What does a kid do when his mum and dad are worry warts? Make them rich, decides Keith. Very, very rich. It's a brilliant plan – if it works. The very funny sequel to *Misery Guts*.

PUPPY FAT

What does a kid do when his mum and dad are past it? Get them into shape, decides Keith. And find them new partners. It's a brilliant plan – but he'll need help. The hilarious and moving sequel to *Misery Guts* and *Worry Warts*.

BELLY FLOP

Mitch needs help. Everyone hates him, but he's got a plan that'll make him the most popular bloke in town. If it doesn't kill him. He's going to have to call on his guardian angel, Doug. If Doug's listening, that is.

AVAILABLE FROM PAN MACMILLAN

ABOUT THE AUTHOR

Morris Gleitzman grew up in England and came to Australia when he was sixteen.

He was a frozen-chicken thawer, sugar-mill rolling-stock unhooker, fashion-industry trainee, student, department-store Santa, TV producer, newspaper columnist and screenwriter. Then he had a wonderful experience. He wrote a novel for young people. Now he's one of Australia's most popular children's authors.

Toad Surprise is his twenty-eighth book.

Visit Morris at his website:
morrisgleitzman.com